The Race
of Our Times

by

Alex Conway

Published by New Generation Publishing in 2024

Copyright © Alex Conway, 2024

First Edition

The author asserts the moral right under the Copyright, Designs and Patents Act 1988 to be identified as the author of this work.

All Rights reserved. No part of this publication may be reproduced, stored in a retrieval system or transmitted, in any form or by any means without the prior consent of the author, nor be otherwise circulated in any form of binding or cover other than that which it is published and without a similar condition being imposed on the subsequent purchaser.

ISBN: 9781835634073

New Generation Publishing
www.newgeneration-publishing.com

*For Arun, Uma and Dylan.
Three rays of eternal sunshine.*

Chapter One

A wave nestled up to Isra's bare foot. A delicate, foamy wave that snaked around the side of her foot and fell away just below the heel. She glanced at the wave and brushed her fingertips against the fizzing water, admiring the colours and bubbles shimmering.

The air felt humid and sticky today. The kind of air that pushed down on her shoulders and stuck inside her throat like fine dust.

She sat on the beach; legs crossed with the breeze embracing her long, curly hair. She cupped a handful of wet sand and released it through her fingertips, watching each grain fall gently into the shimmering cascade of the beach. The clouds had laid a golden trail across the horizon; thick, dense clouds that glimmered through the lost sun. To the east the golden sheen was wearing off into a melting pot of murky whites and lightened greys. She squinted, thinking she could see a gap in the clouds; a hole where a glimmer of radiant blue was peeking through. She released the last of the sand grains and stood up. *Was it a mirage? A dream?* It was beyond beauty. "Canab!" she whispered.

"Ilhama! Come have this Battati." It was Amiin, shouting from the rocky side of the beach.

Isra pointed to the east. "Do you see it, brother? Look!"
"See what?" Amiin shouted back.

"The blue hole, over there," Isra replied, hopping carefully to the edge of a small ditch where Amiin was standing awkwardly, eating mashed up Bataati potatoes from an aluminum tin with his fingers. He placed the tin on the rocks and looked at his sister, like a teacher beginning a class.

"How long has it been since you saw the beautiful blue, Ilhama?" Amiin asked.

Isra picked the tin off the floor. The tin felt heavy with the gloopy starch of sweet potato. "Over a year I think, can't remember."

"I saw it when I was south, did I not tell you?"

Isra scooped a lump of Battati into her mouth. "When you were with Mauricio?"

"Yes," he replied, pensive.

"Why did you not tell me, brother?"

Amiin looked up at the sky. The fading gold sheen was trickling into a stone-wall carpet. And with it a semblance of life was fading into the clouds. "Why, what is the point?" he replied.

"I want to hear about it. The beautiful, lush blue. Paint me a picture, brother!"

Amiin gushed, dwelling at the heavens. A glint appeared in both of his chocolate eyes. "We watched it for a few seconds. It was just before sunset and the clouds suddenly appeared very thin. And then. Then it came! Blazing through like a wave crashing against the shore. Blue like I have not seen for a long time, Ilhama."

"Like the sea?"

"Much brighter and clearer."

"It's been so long I cannot remember it."

Amiin put a hand through his thinning head of greasy hair. "Mauricio told me about a world, a planet in our solar system that is like ours, with an oppressive cloud covering it all year round. We are lucky in that respect."

"Venus?" Isra replied.

"Yes, how did you know?"

"He told me, also."

A glow came over Amiin's hardened, wind-swept face. "Oh, Mauricio! In his day he saw the stars every night."

Isra handed the tin to Amiin. "These are bland. Can I use the salt I dried out from the seawater?"

"Since when do you need salt?"

"Since I discovered it, it's rather nice."

He grinned. "No going back."

"What do you mean?"

"You won't eat a grain without it."

"But I like it. It fizzles on my tongue."

Amiin took the tin from Isra. The skin of his hands was abrasive, like the rocks around him. He scooped another lump of Batatti from the tin and chewed the potatoes slowly. "This was a big problem for our ancestors you know," he said.

"What was?"

"The salt."

"But don't we need the salt?"

"In moderation."

"It is good for us, no? Like the berries and the lentils and the green vegetables."

"Ilhama, every bit of food has its nutrients. This salt though the elders used excessively and led to all kinds of disease, especially the heart."

"So, my heart will stop working if I eat salt?"

"Not straight away, no."

Isra's eyes tightened close to her nose. She scratched her elbow where a blister was forming. "Then how, brother?"

"It's about this." Amiin swallowed the Batatti and pointed at his tongue. "Taste."

Her expression seemed puzzled. "What about it?"

"The more salt we put in our food the more our tastebuds crave it. It is like an addiction, Ilhama. Better we avoid it for now."

Isra danced over to Amiin and put a hand on his shoulder. A fire of grace was dancing on her face, like a gazelle skipping to a merry beat. Her hair suddenly caught a gust of wind, hanging frozen in the air for seconds. Amiin could see yellow streaks at the tips of her curls. "Oh, brother, it's just a bit of salt!" she grinned, as if she were the parent in the debate.

He took her hand from his shoulder and kissed the cracked skin on her knuckles. "You laugh! Oh, you laugh, Ilhama!"

His gaze suddenly switched to a red dot in the sky, past Isra's right ear. It was rising out of the horizon, coming from the north-east. He held Isra close to his chest, feeling a sharp breeze shooting down his neck. "Wait over there." He pushed Isra towards a rock-face.

"Brother, what is it?"

Amiin stood transfixed at the red dot which was taking a downward trajectory towards the ground. "Just do as I say, wait in the cave. GO!" He turned around. She could see beads of sweat on his forehead. The colour of his face had turned white like the foam of the shore. For a split second she imagined a skeleton talking to her.

"Please go and wait. I will come and get you. And don't worry, I am sure it is nothing."

Isra had seen an identical ghoulish expression wrapped around Amiin's face before. It was a sign of dread. Like a soldier executing an order, Isra nodded and jumped into the ditch. She turned her head whilst swimming in an algae infested rock-pool, to Amiin. Past his head the spot was now lower on the horizon; glowing a phosphorate orange as it raced through the clouds, leaving a trail of white fumes that lit up the grey blanket hanging in the sky. She climbed out of the water and entered through a small hole in the rocks. "What is it?" she said, quivering uncomfortably at the cave entrance.

A delayed rumble like a thunderclap rolled through the sky. The rumble fizzed and popped as the dot disappeared beyond the horizon. Amiin looked to the ground. His feet shook acutely. He turned and clambered up the rock wall that surrounded the cave. As he climbed his foot collided with the sharp edge of a rock and blood spurted from the underside of his foot. He jumped down from the rocky incline to the entrance of the cave, tracing the direction where the fireball had landed. "Not so long-ago Mauricio said it was a messenger you knew."

"I remember," she replied from within the cave walls.

Amiin turned into the cave entrance, where light met dark and dry met damp air. The whites of Isra's eyes appeared. "You do?" he said.

"Brother, he said all sorts of craziness that day. He was

hallucinating strange things." Her feet then appeared in the light, wrinkled, and scratched like an old leather bag.

"Didn't we find the well the next day?"

"The well! Mauricio said it was five years and no water." She shuffled her body next to Amiin on the damp rocks. "He thought it was some kind of sign. That we would find water."

Amiin poked his head out of the cave. His face twitched. "The old fool!"

He picked a small rock from the floor of the cave and threw it into the deepest part of the rock pool. As the stone collided with the water he listened intently once the stone had sunk to the bottom of the pool. An eerie silence prevailed.

He sat down on a flattened rock outside of the cave, looking at the blood trickling from his foot. A wound no more than an inch, deep into the flesh. He prodded the wound with his finger. A drop of sweat dripped from his nose onto the rocks. *This was the day! When the signals in the sky would be answered,* he thought.

"Has the messenger arrived?" Isra whispered.

Amiin looked into her jittery eyes; two points releasing red streams of plasma into the outer shell that was her corneas. Her very own solar winds.

"I think so," he whispered.

Chapter Two

That evening once the moon appeared behind the wall of clouds, Amiin grabbed a large green rucksack from the cave and threw in their belongings: two mess tins, some drawings of their mother, three pashminas, some dirty linen, a pair of cotton trousers, two plastic spoons, four ragged shirts, an empty butane gas canister, clothes pegs, a long tarpaulin sheet, food tins, four wooden pegs, a cotton dress, three water canisters and a small silver ornament. The ornament was in the shape of a flame, with a family huddled together at the bottom of the flame, expressionless. It was passed onto Amiin from his mother before her death. As he placed the ornament into a zipped pocket, he recalled her words while she lay on the beach, bloodshot in the eye with luminance dripping from her skin waiting for death:

"Take this, my boy."
"What is it?" Amiin replied.
"It is from your father."
"What do I do with it?"

His mother coughed blood onto the sand, while the moonlight glistened against her teeth. She was shivering like a fish out of water. "If all else seems lost remember you will have your sister. She will be your strength and you will be hers. This will remind you, when you need reminding that this is your life, take it. No matter how hard you think it is, take it!"

Isra lay on her back; eyes glued shut, skin crinkled like a piece of paper crushed. Their mother lay silent on the beach gazing up at the stars who had penetrated through the clouds. In these years, the clouds were thinner; making the stars appear like glow-worms, slowly crawling along the ever-widening branches of the Milky Way.

Her breathing became shallow: "Markaan Da'da jirey shan iyo toban markaan damac guur lasoo kacey," she sung, with an earnest effort.

Amiin touched his mother on the cheek, kissed her on the forehead then leant over and grasped his new-born sister in his arms. He cradled her in his shirt, then carefully un-buttoned his shirt until her sapped, oily skin was covered in the fabric. He then turned to face his mother, but she had stopped breathing...

A heightened yelp suddenly zipped across the sand. It was a mongrel puppy-dog, who had been hanging around the beach, scavenging for food and a semblance of company. Isra was tying her hair into a tight ponytail.

"What do we do about the little plum?" she said hesitantly.

The puppy appeared like halcyon projectors, unpanicked. "We don't have time, Ilhama."

Isra forlornly looked at the puppy. "Don't have time for what?"

"We don't have time for passengers."

"Passengers?"

Amiin tied the top of the rucksack with a frayed piece of string "Yes, passengers. We must leave."

"But leave where?"

"Stop asking questions and just listen to me will you!"

Isra glanced at the puppy, at the shades of sandy brown blending into white and black patches on its coat. Ears scrambled by the dry heat and innocuous, delicate eyes extinguished in the smog of the beach, where she stood. "Leave the little plum, brother? Leave him here?"

"Yes, we must, Ilhama."

"But why must we?"

"Damn, Ilhama, this is not like one of those stories where the long-lost animal joins the flock and finds a home. This is survival! Do you know what is out there?"

Isra flinched her jaw and turned away from the puppy. A glimmer of claret bubbles nestled in the side of her vision.

"You are going to tell me it is for the best. That we need to be mean."

Amiin nestled up to Isra and held her close to his chest. "It is for the best."

"To keep running?" her lips squashed up to Amiin's chest hair. "But why do we need to keep running?"

"We are not running. This is life. This is who we are."

Isra turned away from her brother's sweaty chest hair. Her eyes were tingling, mouth wide open. The puppy was staring straight at her, as if an arrow pointed in her direction "Life?" she said, despondently.

Amiin ran a finger through his sister's tangled hair. She looked like a desert queen, arisen from the egg of a scorpion. "This is life I'm afraid."

She jumped out of Amiin's grasp onto the damp, clumpy sand in between the rocks. Then tied her ponytail tighter and flicked her wrist at the puppy. "Shoo!" she yelled. "Shoo!"

A crackle echoed in the distance, like a thunderclap. "Let's go," Amiin said.

Isra grabbed the last of the food tins out of the cave and stowed them in the rucksack. Amiin then threw the rucksack over his shoulders as they left the beach behind. Isra turned one last time before they descended out of the cliff towards the desert. The puppy had disappeared. Isra turned her ears towards the sea, the calming hush of waves hitting the shore. Not a yelp was heard.

"Run ahead like we did before, no more than fifty yards from me," Amiin said as he wiped sweat from his forehead. He looked beyond to the sea in front of him. Not the sea of water but the sea of desert. The humidity pressed down on his shoulders as he took the first step downhill.

Isra ran in front of Amiin then stopped abruptly. On the floor nestled to a pile of aluminum cans and rocks was a small pair of binoculars. Amiin took the binoculars and placed them into his trouser pocket, unsure what they were. "I trust you, brother" Isra whispered into the winds.

For days they continued into the lands where white sands

merged into white clouds. This was the desert — the real desert; oppressive and unforgiving; punctuated only by hardy shrubs and baked rocks where small lizards and scorpions scuttled in and out.

Their senses seemed to hang still in the parched air; smells became distant, water from their canisters had little taste, their sight was blurry. The only sound they could hear was the howling of the wind at night. They passed carcasses of goats and camels, stuck to the sand like flies on dripping paper while above the vultures hovered. Amiin looked at the vultures frequently, for it was the only semblance of life he could now reference beside himself and Isra. *What could these scavenger birds see beyond the desert? To the lands beyond the Arabian sea? And what did these birds drink in this arid wilderness?* Their lives seemed easy in the sky looking down on the world.

Amiin hobbled behind Isra. The cut on his foot had healed but was sore to walk on. "Ilhama!" he shouted. His voice was coarse. "Let us stop over there by that camel. We can use the sheet for shade."

Isra turned around. The beige cotton dress she was wearing appeared brighter against the gleaming sand. "But why do we need shade? There is no sun."

"The UV rays that is why. Remember what I told you?"

Isra signalled to Amiin in a gesture of compliance. Something then caught her eye on the ground, in between a small cactus and a scattering of clumpy sand. It was a small iron object, triangular with a rusty brown colour. She picked it up. "Ow!"

"What's the matter, Ilhama?"

"It's really hot!"

Isra looked down at the piece of rusted metal. "Strange. What is it?"

"Looks like an arrow-tip. Could be old. Thousands of years old."

Isra gawped down at the artefact "Wow! Really?"

"Pick it up with some cloth and stow it away for now."

"What could it be?"

"Mau would have had his theories, I'm sure." He dropped the rucksack by the skeleton of the long-deceased camel, touching the ribcage of the skeleton. It was silky smooth, almost oily. He glanced at the skeleton, ghosting a shadow across the desert. The carrion had disappeared into the belly of desert dogs and vultures long ago. He closed his eyes for a second and imagined a group of nomads roaming the desert; two camels, four humans, and their possessions tied to the camel's humps. Sorrow and regret would have filled the stifling air the day they had to leave this wondrous mammal for the biggest element of nature, sitting high in the sky. He turned around to where Isra's find lay, wondering if the camel and arrow were connected.

He opened his eyes. "It would have been a slow death for this one," he murmured.

Isra sat in a corner of the shade, near the camel's backbone. "It's definitely a camel?"

"Yes, it is."

"We don't see them so much now."

Amiin turned to the skull, like he was looking the mammal straight in the eye. "The meat would have been precious."

"To eat?"

"Why, yes. Meat is meat."

She faced Amiin "Ugh! Camel meat must be dry and tough like old shoes."

He looked down at the shrouded pieces of leather that covered his feet, remembering the day he had bartered with the cobbler in the town of Bosaso. The cobbler demanded ten bronze and he only had three. A compromise was made with some palladium metal he had found inside two glass devices found on the side of the road. The devices, which he had seen strewn across the land were becoming valuable when it came to metals, with traders using magnifying glasses to extract the metals from within.

A sharp breeze blew into Isra's face, lifting her fringe into the air. He noticed a purple vein protruding from her brow.

"It is so hot out here, I forgot how much. My feet feel like they are melting into the ground," she said.

He rummaged through the rucksack, pulling out the tarpaulin sheet and three poles. The sheet unraveled, blowing in the wind like the sail on a small dinghy. He put one pole through the ribcage of the skeleton and another through what looked like a thighbone. He shook at the poles secured against the silky marrow, then threw the last pole into the sand. "Damn, it's hot against the sand!" he said.

"Let me try…" Isra threw the pole into the sandy earth like a stake. "…not sure how this will hold, though."

Her cheeks flushed as she pushed down on the pole with all her strength. Amiin took his shoe off and battered the pole with the foot-sole until all he could see was a stump. "Bend it a bit more so we can get the string on an angle."

The pole poked out of the ground at a jaunty angle. Amiin then tied the string around the it and threw a hole in the sheet. The sheet flapped loosely in the wind, as if it were soaking the solar bursts. "Get under," he said to Isra.

Isra was sweating profusely, from elbow to brow. She hid under the sheet. "Brother, I still do not see why we need protection from the clouds. There is no sunshine."

Amiin nestled up to Isra under the sheet. He spat sand from his mouth. "We still need shelter for lots of reasons, Ilhama. Not just from the sun, sandstorms, the coldness of night. Besides, it's cooler under here don't you think?"

Isra's face blushed. "Okay, it is."

"We should stay here the night."

"How far do we go?"

Amiin sighed a familiar sigh. One of having to explain unfortunate events once again. "You know how far."

"No, I don't."

"What have you been taught?"

"That home does not exist. Only shelter."

"And what else?"

Isra's eyes glazed over, wetted. "That we must travel until we find food and water. That we must travel to find shelter and listen to our siblings for whispers, keep an ear to the ground."

"And what do you think that racket was? Coming from the east – an angel?"

"Something not good."

"Exactly. We move. That is what we do."

"I know."

"We'll move until we find the..."

"...the next shelter. You do not have to keep reminding me."

Isra turned her back on Amiin. The tip of her hair was shaped like an anchor. He stroked the tip of her coarse hair, then felt around in the pocket of the rucksack and pulled out a wristwatch: 07:11PM the display read. Isra then fell asleep while Amiin gazed longingly at the back of her head, for answers. *What was the real reason to keep moving? How safe was it?* He wished he could open a book and look up the answers.

He felt restless so pulled his body out from the cover and into the sandy winds. The light was starting to fade, trickling a copper sheen towards the west that made the clouds look like spots of dirt. He pulled his face towards the breeze, feeling a tickle of grit on the side of his face as his eyes closed to the dusk. All was silent in the desert, except for the slight howl of the wind.

Then, a tinge of an echo crossed his ears, a tingle in the distance. The sound pitched high in his register sounding familiar, like a bell. It rang into the wind then dissipated. The sound arrived again, tingling. He opened his eyes, to the fading light of bronze desert. It was a bell. One like the goat herders that came to market every week looking to trade milk for rice, cotton, fruits, even tools. He cupped his eyes as if makeshift binoculars were in his hands and scanned the desert to where the bell sound was coming from.

In the near distance he made out a figure lumbering in the sand, dressed head to toe in a thick Haik. The figure was guiding two goats in front with a stick. Trailing behind the shadow of the Haik, a smaller figure appeared. Amiin squinted his eyes but could only see a red blush of some kind of dress, simmering against the fading light.

The bell of the goats tinkled. As they drew near Amiin made out a beard under the Haik, for a moment he thought of Mauricio. He looked to the clouds and felt a tinge of sadness.

"Waxaa jira joojin lahaa!" the man in the Haik shouted. Amiin looked over the man's shoulder to the smaller figure in the red clothing. It was a girl with long, sandy brown hair that was blowing either side of her shoulders.

Isra emerged, standing next to Amiin.

"Friend or foe?" she said.

"We'll find out soon enough."

The goats veered off to the side of the skeleton and stood still. Their eyes were like marbles, as still as the mountains. "Joogi! Joogi!" the man said, and the bell chimes ceased. The goat-herder stopped ten feet in front of Amiin and Isra.

Amiin extended his arm and raised his hand. The man twiddled with the stick then raised his arm, like he was embracing the air.

"Salan! Greetings!" Amiin said, keeping an eye on the circumspect child behind.

The goat-herder nodded, releasing the hood of his Haik. His face was sun-burnt auburn, with thick lines indented into his forehead. Around his ears wispy hair as dusty as the sand blew, curving and coiling around the back of his head like a pair of enormous ears. "Where have you come from?" he asked.

"The coast," Amiin replied.

"Which coast?"

"The Aden coast. Near to Lughaya."

The man kicked the stick and immediately settled to the floor. Knees, like tiny stones appeared from under the Haik. "Lughaya, eh? I thought that place went to the dogs long ago." The girl walked up behind the man, gently tiptoeing along the sand barefoot. He signalled with a shaking motion of his right hand and the girl stopped, staring blankly into the distance.

"So why here? All I can see are sand and winds and death for you coastal folk."

Amiin looked at the girl, then at the goats. He had a strange premonition that the goats would attack them both and suck their eyeballs dry. "We heard the noise," he replied.

"The noise of chaos, eh? Get it out here too, you know, boy."

"It felt close, so we took off. I am Amiin by the way. This is Is—"

"Pssst!" cried the goat-herder. "Pssst!"

The girl emerged from the red covers and sat down next to him. Her face glimmered in the sunset, like moonlight on the sea. As she glided along the sand the outline of her legs appeared, reedy like bamboo shoots.

The goat-herder placed his hand into the Haik and produced a small piece of bark. "Amiin, you say. And who is this?" He chewed on the bark silently.

"Isra," she hushed.

"Isamah?"

"No, Issssraaaah."

He took the bark from his mouth. "Isra? Sounds Abyssinian. How are you little one?"

The goat-herder tossed the bark around his mouth, his gaze solely fixed on Isra.

Isra cowered behind Amiin, clinging to his trousers. "What brings you around these parts then...?" Amiin cupped his hand into a welcoming gesture.

"Mousa. Mousa the goat."

"You or the goat?"

"I am Mousa."

"But you said the goat."

Mousa turned to the girl. "Tuh! Young folk. Cannot differentiate."

The girl stood up and backed away, the red of her dress forming a glossy pattern against the sandy earth "Salan! And you are?" Amiin moved his hand towards the girl who looked around forlorn, like a rabbit parading around an inhospitable plain. She stared expressionless back at Amiin. Amiin saw for the first-time freckles dashed around her glossy eyes, sparkling like crystals.

Isra appeared by Amiin's thigh in sight of Mousa. "Well, Mousa, where are you heading?" Amiin asked.

The man called Mousa got to his knees and picked up the stick. The outline of his face silhouetted against the clouds, lighting his teeth up into orange flames. "We trail behind the goats. These are the saviors, the ones who will lead us to fresh water as clear as the mountain stream and wheat blowing gently in the field."

"So, you are following the goats?"

"No, I am their master."

"Why don't you just eat them?"

Mousa paced back and forth while the girl paced backwards. "Eat the goats you say. Just for their meat?"

"Their meat could sustain you for weeks, Mousa."

"Never… NEVER!"

"But you and your companion look very hungry."

The girl took shy steps towards Amiin. "What is your name?" he asked.

Mousa yanked at the girl's wrist, pulling her back behind him. Her eyes suddenly jolted, to a stern, rigid facade. The shimmering lights of freckles quickly disappeared.

"Mary," replied Mousa, agitated.

"Mary? Not from these parts," replied Amiin.

"Biblical," said Isra.

Amiin turned to Isra who was drawing shapes in the sand with her toes. "It is a biblical name."

Mousa swung his stick to the ground. "What does it matter about her name? Look, can we help each other or not? Otherwise, we shall be on our way."

A sharp, chilly breeze brushed along the ground, whipping sand into Amiin's face. The sand felt hard and frosty, like hail stones. He looked to the horizon where the sun was about to set. He could barely make out the last glimpses of sunlight fighting through the dense forest of clouds. "We do not have much. Just this cover for shelter and clothes. Basic rations, some water. But you can stay with us if you wish."

Mousa stepped to within a few feet of Amiin. He smelt tangy, the smell of the desert. He then turned to where the goats were resting. Bones were jutting out of the side of their bodies and their bellies had no sag at all, just a flat-lined piece of tissue. They stared listlessly into the great mass that had always been their home, the sprawling mass of sand and death; the very land that would one day swallow up all of Africa, so the prophets would say.

Mousa and the girl camped with them that night. Through the night the fading echoes of rumbling breezed across the land; sequestered, isolated bursts that dipped in and out of the howling wind.

Amiin opened his eyes and snuggled up next to Isra who was asleep. He then peered through Isra's hair where Mousa lay next to sticks burning, his body covered in a thick woven blanket. His crooked nose poked out of the blanket, bulbous and red in the firelight. The goats rested close to Mousa with the same doleful expression that screamed of prolonged fate, one that Amiin could recognise, even in a goat.

Mousa did not seem asleep, he gazed intently at a faded star that had joined them for the night. The girl's legs appeared next to Mousa, shivering, and shaking awkwardly. Mousa put a hand on the legs and the shivering immediately stopped. He whispered to the girl then lay on his back, staring vehemently at the pallid speck of light in the sky about to disappear.

Chapter Three

In the morning as soon as the sunlight had brazed her lips through the tarpaulin sheet, Isra awoke. She peaked out from under the sheet, looking out for red dots in the sky. She listened intently for explosions in the distance but could hear none.

The first noise of revile came from the goats, rustling their hooves against the scraggy floor and spluttering a wild cough into the cooling air.

Isra left Amiin asleep on the floor, nestled up to the thigh bone of the camel. She closed her eyes and wrapped a pashmina scarf around her neck, the silence of dawn. She always liked this time of day. Closing her eyes and opening her nostrils she would breathe in the air of another day, imagining thousands upon thousands of years ago when the first Homo-sapiens walked this very piece of land. Their senses finely tuned to the beats and the rhythm of nature, survival like now; sleep, eat, drink, sleep, eat, drink. Awaken the next day.

She had heard stories about the first variations of humans evolving out of this land. How they had evolved from monkeys into hunters, then making settlements, growing food, killing each over land. Then this thing called the 'technological revolution' which connected to light in houses, weapons that could kill thousands of people, how they travelled and connected with each other. The devices littered on the ground clues as to how it all worked. The fuel to power these slim, rectangle boxes had run out, she had been told. But parts of the world still used them to talk to each other, sell things, buy things, play games, to even find out about the news. It all seemed weird to her.

Mousa's head appeared out of the sheet, shaking, and

turning as if fleas had infested his scalp. He grabbed the stick and jolted upwards, mumbling incoherently to the goats. Isra watched Mousa in the increasing light, towering over the landscape in the Haik like a tall, spindly tree. His hair appeared greasier than yesterday, with less curls, more matting as he fumbled the stringy clumps into a ponytail.

She could see heavy lines indented into his face, lines as thick as cracks in the earth. He turned towards Isra and smiled. Isra looked away towards the goats and fiddled with her scarf. She grinned. It felt nice having companions today.

"Ilhama, are you awake?" Amiin said. His voice muffled from under the sheet.

"Yes, brother," she replied, startled.

"Why do you keep waking so early?"

"Because... because..." She picked stones from the floor and threw them in the air. "I like the smell of a new day."

Amiin's head peaked out of the side of the sheet. "Cannot be past six. Get some rest."

"I'm not tired."

His face was carrying the creases of sleep, worn heavily into the fabric of his walnut skin. He squinted at Isra then turned towards Mousa who was giving the goats water from a canister.

"Stay close. Do not wander off do you hear! We will set off in the next hours."

Amiin's head retreated under the sheet, like a snail hiding in its warm, safe shell. He rested his head back onto the side of the rucksack, threw a blanket over his chest and tried to get back to sleep. This time in the morning he always felt guilty if Isra was awake, as if he should be doing something, rustling up some kind of breakfast, brushing his teeth with the same revolting mint water or plotting a route for the day. *It could wait!* he thought. His eyes drifted, his body feeling heavy and tied to the floor.

He awoke an hour later, dazed, with a pinging sensation in the bottom of his stomach.

"Brother, quick. See! Come see!" Isra shook the sheet

violently, then tapped on Amiin's shoulders. He threw the blanket to the floor and rushed out into the open.

"What? What is it, Ilhama?!" he mumbled, blowing vapor into the morning air.

He could see Isra and Mousa both standing still, like concrete pillars. Isra seemed to have grown overnight, almost to Mousa's chin. Her disposition one of awe, with hands twitching by her side, her chin silhouetting against the last remnants of night. He followed the line of Isra's chin to the red ball in the sky heading downwards. The ball was close, with a foaming tail that resembled a mushroom.

"Is that what I think it is?" said Mousa.

Amiin moved beside Mousa. The hardened, brazen looks of the wilderness had immersed into halcyon white eyes, a drooping bottom lip and a quivering of the hands. The ball gathered speed and settled past the horizon to the south-east. "Well, that depends. Tell me what you think it is?" Amiin replied.

"The messengers."

Amiin felt a ping of joy, like he had one up on the wily goat-herder. "Messengers from where… Arabia? Italia?" A rumbling echo pierced the deathly silence of the desert, reverberating from ear to ear. He turned to Isra.

First the crack ripped through the ground. Then the whip of the missile crashing to the floor vibrated the soles of his feet. The girl, Mary, appeared from Mousa's shadow, gazing in wonderment at the cloud of blood red smoke rising like a volcano cloud over the desert horizon. While Mousa stepped back from the explosion in the distance, Mary moved towards it, holding Mousa's stick. Mousa ran after Mary, grabbed the stick, and struck her with an open palm around the back of the head.

"Are you mad? Get back, you silly creature," Mousa barked.

Mary scampered back towards the camel skeleton, covering her face from Mousa's steely glare. Mousa waved his hands towards the skeleton, like he was hushing away an annoying fly. His cheeks had turned rubicund.

Amiin looked at Mary who was leaning behind the camel's backbone. Her body was curled around the bone, like a scorpion. She looked scared. *What a strange creature,* he thought. Her eyes dotted around the desert, scattergun and without a point of focus.

In those few seconds Amiin watched her walk up to the explosion he imagined Carissa: The Queen of the Desert with a legion of snakes by her side. Carissa, legend had it, was the daughter of Bedouin peasants from the Western Sahara hundreds of years ago. The family wandered nomadically for years, taking shelter in the towns and farms that dotted the sand swept roads cutting through the Sahara like thinning arteries. Carissa's father Jamol worked as a straw-roof builder, finding work from town to town until one day the baking heat became unbearable and he collapsed by the road from a weak heart. "Help!" Carissa's mother Mariam shouted. "Help!" There was nobody within sight. He died within minutes — leaving a grief-stricken wife and a six-year-old daughter. Despite the loss and the anguish of losing their father Mariam wiped her tears, picked Carissa up and continued regardless in the face of the mother god — the sun.

Carissa and her mother did not know where to go and felt abandoned. They stopped in refuges near the last drops of what was Lake Chad; tin hut's, sandstone abodes or disbanded cars dotted along the roads.

They lived like this for weeks, vagabonds of the wasteland. Then one day in the town of Blablin, Mariam befriended a man called Djarma, with a gentle face and hair as wild as thorn bushes. He approached the two of them one day when her mother was overcome with heat exhaustion and offered to carry their bags to the next village. Overcome with delirium and a dizzying sense of the skies falling in on her, Mariam agreed, and they stayed the night in the man's ramshackle hut. In the morning Mariam awoke with blood gushing from her vagina and Carissa did not know why. She fled with her daughter from the filthy abode where the rape had taken place; murmurings of groaning and floorboards creaking ringing in her mother's ears.

Mariam was never the same again after that day. It was like her heart had been ripped out of her throat. Three hard months later while they were staying in a disused Millet farm-barn Mariam cut her wrists with a carving skewer and was gone to join her husband in the afterlife. Carissa was now just seven years old. She buried her mother's body with not an ounce of sorrow or bitterness towards her. Her mother could not go on, there was no more to say. So, Carissa threw the shovel into the sandy earth, took a big sup of water from the lake, and wandered headfirst along the old remnants of Lake Chad and north past Mousorro into the badlands of the South Sahara. She would march on her own, followed by an army of sand-snakes through the dust like a queen shimmering into the homeland. One day the heat also took her to the ground. The snakes stopped that day and curled up by her side. Hundreds of snakes, giving way to the perishing heat. All they could find of her under the pile of dead snake carcasses was a bronze amulet, inscribed with: ALSHAMS YUQARIR MASIRANA (THE SUN OUR GOD DECIDES OUR FATE).

Carissa was no queen or heavenly spirit. She was nothing more than a little girl, living on borrowed time. But her spirit lived on through the Saharan people for generations.

They quickly packed away their belongings and left the camel's skeleton, heading in a southerly direction. Amiin took the lead, pointing Mousa and the goats in the direction he thought would bring safety and shelter. But all the while he was now guessing, hoping, and guessing again. He looked ahead to the jilted horizon; the clouds were dense and puffy, and the perishing daylight crowded the expanse of desert around them, penning them in like cattle to a tight fence. A wind picked up, blowing his cotton top around his mouth.

He moved the long-sleeved top to one side. "How many cans of beans do we have?"

"Two on last count," replied Isra. "What about them?" she pointed behind at the lagging, lumbering bodies of Mousa and Mary in the distance. The goats were hardly visible in the dust and bright light.

"Let's keep it a mean ration; think we may need it."

Isra turned around. "What about that lot?"

Amiin bit his bottom lip, exposing a top tooth of yellowing worn brusque. "They have their means."

"What means is that. Did you see their poor flesh, brother? It was barely hanging to the bone."

He grabbed Isra by the shoulders. "God be you, Ilhama, this is not about them, this is about us." He spat on the reddening, baked ground. "Can't you see? This is us against the elements, just us. And we MUST survive no matter what, for the sake of mother, our beautiful mother — the Carissa of our time! Can't you see? She died to bring us here and we must honour her memory. WE MUST GO ON!"

Isra shook her shoulders and released Amiin's loosening grip. Her eyes resilient and masterful in condemnation. "Why must we go on, brother?"

A red glow reflected from Isra's pupils; a glow of the sun Amiin had not seen before. It was like a fire fanning across the desert, resolute in all its destruction of the landscape colonised. The hints of turquoise in her eyes, like the Arabian Sea that he had swum in as a child, seemed to distinguish into a haze of hellfire and smoking palm trees that blazed a path before him.

He threw the rucksack on the floor. "Stop questioning me, please."

"But why? What is before us? I feel very tired."

He grabbed Isra's bony arm, puffing in the oppressive, muggy heat. "Let us live our life."

Isra twisted her body out of Amiin's grip. "I may be your younger sister who does not know much about the world, but I do not see this as living, brother. This is surviving," said Isra.

"In order to live you must first survive," he stuttered back.

Isra turned her back to Amiin and folded her arms. She looked at the goats wandering aimlessly along the landscape with the bell tinkle reverberating along the flat lands. A tear ran along the side of her face and dropped to the floor. "I don't think I have the strength, brother."

"What are the options then? WHAT ARE OUR OPTIONS, OH SAGE SISTER?" Amiin screamed, almost pulling a lung.

She turned towards Amiin and held his hand. He looked exhausted, panting, like a dog. She widened her mouth and smiled at her brother. There was something hiding under his protective sheen she sensed, some kind of guilt hiding.

"Brother, you need to tell me what we are running from."

He sat on the rucksack and rubbed his hair. Isra could see dust flying out of his scalp. He coughed and looked at Isra, pensive. "When we find shelter, I will tell you."

That night in amongst a stack of boulders that had appeared magically in the desert, they camped. Amiin had spotted the pile of rocks from a fair distance as their smooth surfaces beamed against the moonlight. The sheet was thrown up across two of the boulders and tied to some shrubs. They curled up underneath as the sheet flapped in the wind helplessly, almost calling for help. A whistling sound breezed around the other side of the boulders where Mousa, Mary and the goats lay under the blanket of clouds sleeping.

The air was fresh and chilly, enough to make the hairs on the back of Amiin's neck stand tall as the morning came. He finished eating a dried cob of corn and threw the finished cob out to the goats. Isra sat up, with an intensity of purpose burnishing her retinas. She pulled away from a pile of blankets and touched Amiin on the arm. "Now tell me."

"Tell you what?" Amiin replied, spitting out the remnants of the dried corn. "Finish your corn."

Isra placed the cob on a dirty piece of cloth. "Brother, you cannot keep playing the wise one all your life. I am old enough to understand. You promised!"

Amiin realised that this was the crossroads, no turning back. The moment he had been dreading since Isra's birth when he would have to inform his younger sister that they were both small, insignificant specks of dust floating around a polluted, broken world and that their futures were very unclear. From this moment Isra would turn from the innocent girl into the tough, granite jawed young woman with no room for sentiment or praise or room in her heart for passion. This was his fear. The world would grab her now and hold her in its grasp until the rites of passage had been drilled into her cranium with brutal efficiency.

He held her hand and looked her flat in the eye. "I cannot be sure — rockets, I think. Or maybe flares."

"Rockets? Why would there be rockets? Is there an army?"

"An army of sorts but not one of tanks or ships."

"Then what is that in the sky?"

"I cannot be sure. We do not want to go near it. It could be a trap."

Isra fidgeted with her nails, picking out dirt with the longest nail. "But why?"

"They are trying to find people like us. To entice us."

"So, we join them?"

"Yes."

"So, we follow the red dots, and they take us in?"

"Yes."

"Will there be shelter and food and clean water?"

"I do not know, Ilhama. We are safer here."

Isra pulled her arm away from Amiin, as if she were severing a chain. She glanced over at one of the goats, dolefully licking the husk of corn. She then stood up, looking disorientated. "Safer here?"

"Yes, we are safer here."

"Brother, we are miles from the nearest town with hardly any food or water. And my feet are very sore."

"Each other, that is what we have. And nobody telling us how to live."

"But what good is that if we die out here?"

"We will not die out here. Look at Mousa and Mary, they

are still alive, aren't they? Do they look like people who have submitted?"

Isra shook her head. "I see corpses roaming the wilderness."

Amiin ran a hand through his hair. "Trust me, Ilhama, we are better off here," he said.

"Who told you they were rockets?"

"A few people."

"Who?"

"Mauricio, among others."

"Ha! And you now believe the crazy old fool. Not so long ago he was a heretic, a madman you said!"

"It makes sense. They need us more than we need them."

Isra kicked at the loose gravel around the base of the boulders. A scorpion suddenly scuttled out of the rocks, raising its pincers in the air. She waved her hands. "Psssst!" she shouted. "Psssst!"

Her eyebrows arched as she watched the scorpion scuttle into the open ground and turned its pincers towards Mousa and Mary. The scorpion's tail then curled tight into a ball as its claws shrunk into the shadow cast by the rock. "Psssst!"

"What a beautiful thing you are," Amiin said, with the air of grace.

"Beautiful? He is after us look at him!" Isra replied. "Mousa, Mary. Look! Look!"

"Ilhama, it will not hurt you. Anyone would think you hadn't seen a scorpion before."

"Creatures of hell is what they are."

Mousa appeared from behind the rock face, swinging the stick at the scorpion. "Be gone. Go! Go!" he yelled. His pupils were dilated. "I do not like scorpions. They bring us bad luck." Out of his hand a bunch of chaat leaves appeared. He tore off a leaf and chewed on it. The scorpion stood its ground, hissing.

"Oh, brother, make it go, make it go! It is scaring me," Isra cried.

"You have scared it, is all. Was minding its own business."

Mousa waved the stick nearer the scorpion, almost catching it by the tail. Then out of Mousa's shadow, Mary appeared for the first time that morning.

Amiin glanced at Mary. The outline of her body shimmered like a flame tossed about in the wind. Her hair was tied into a tight bun which revealed a pale stretch of skin lining the upper side of her forehead. And for the first time he noticed traces of indigo buried deep into her eyes. "The scorpion will not hurt us," she hushed.

"Sit down and attend to the goats," said Mousa.

"They will not," Mary replied.

"I SAID..." Mousa's voice deepened.

Mary disappeared behind the shadow of Mousa. She sat solemnly, laying hay on the floor for the goats. The goats leapt up, devouring the hay as she stroked the back of their heads. Her gaze stared towards the horizon, to the reddened patches of clouds. Amiin turned to the horizon, where the sun was lighting up the desert. This time of morning the ground and the horizon appeared like a staircase, a ladder of colours ascending into a blush, flecked hue. The goats continued to munch on the hay, the chomping and clattering of teeth the only sounds in the stillness of paranormal time.

"Ilhama, no!" Amiin pushed Isra out of the way. "What are you doing? Its sting is deadly."

"I… I just wanted to pick it up and show it the way."

"The way where?"

"To safety."

"He does not need our help. Do you know how long these creatures have been around?"

The scorpion's tail straightened, revealing a line of scales in a trail of plum tints. Isra moved away from the scorpion. She investigated the small black dots on the scorpion's face; a pair of eyes that had survived and worn the ages. Then she looked at the rock from where the creature had crawled out from, noticing lines and rings curving around the circumference. The same rings of time that were in the

DNA of this creature standing pensively beneath her feet. Her expression quickly wilted.

Mousa stood motionless as the scorpion turned sideways, moving its shelled legs into the vast expanse that lay before them, evermore.

"Where will it go? There is nothing here," asked Isra.

Mary emerged once again. "Longer than us. Longer than the apes, even the dinosaurs."

Isra wiped dust from her eyes and licked her lips which were bristling pink in the daylight. "What was that?" she said, turning toward Mary.

Mary looked away from Isra, bashfully catching a glimpse of Amiin. "The scorpions."

"What about them, oh quiet one?"

"Their ancestors have roamed the planet for millions of years. Four hundred and thirty million I have heard."

"Tuh! You could say that about the humans," Isra turned to Amiin. "What were we called?"

"Neanderthals," Amiin replied.

"Neanderthals. Yes. Seen pictures of them — really ugly looking people."

Amiin smirked, jovially. "I told you before, Ilhama, they were not like us. They were shorter with hunched backs and a different skeleton. They also had smaller brains."

"How do you know this?"

"They found their skulls buried in the ground, a long time ago."

Mary looped around Amiin, like a prairie dog circling around an angry snake. She turned her back on them both, staring into the distance at the dot rubbing the desert floor with rogue flecks. "The Neanderthals came from apes who many millions of years before lived in the sea, but the scorpions were scuttling around and surviving even before the dinosaurs."

"Rubbish! Where did you hear such nonsense? They must have changed over the years," said Amiin.

Mary turned around. "I just know," she said, quietly.

"Enough of this nonsense. We must move! I feel a chill in the air." Mousa hit the stick hard on a rock. He ran up to Mary and shook her by the shoulders, then turned towards Amiin glaringly. "Scorpions! Who cares if they have been around for a billion years? We must look at ourselves and how WE survive, friends."

Amiin turned to Mousa. His expression had changed overnight, from haughty to anxiety. His eyes had a glaze on them. Amiin could see a cry for help for the first time in the wiry old goat-herder. "Let her go," Amiin said.

Mousa loosened his grip on Mary's shoulders and brushed her fringe away from her eyes. "I am just looking out for you, little one. We will get on, but we must be together. Always! Like the heart to the brain, we must be connected, otherwise what else is there?" He knelt down and tightened his grip around her shoulders, this time harder than before as his nails dug into her shoulders like talons.

"You do believe me, don't you?" Mousa pleaded. He then whispered into Mary's ear and withdrew his grip. Mary's expression resembling the face of a stone sculpture from an ancient civilisation withering through time.

They packed away their belongings and set off within the hour, almost bending their path to where the scorpion had escaped to.

Chapter Four

A long month passed for Isra, Amiin, and their new companions. Their tongues, conditioned to the dryness in the air craved moisture. Isra and Amiin sipped on their water cannisters tepidly, every step harder as their bodies shrivelled in the baking heat.

Isra suggested they venture into an abandoned habitation. They had no choice by now; the air was becoming drier, filled with sand-flies, and choking dust. Isra continually fainted in the heat. Weeks ago, Mousa was able to guide them to wells in the ground, guided by a sense. It was like he could sniff the water underground. But there was a problem with the water the further they ventured into the desert. It was becoming murkier and tasted metallic. And the lack of clean water was pulling blood from the bowels of Mousa.

Amiin could feel hunger pinching at his veins. Every morning, he would roll out, from layers of sheets, onto the hard, rocky floor and hallucinate that today they would find a supply of delicious food, freshly cooked on a table, on a sheet as white as snow. Lamb was his favourite; cooked in tomatoes, garlic and spices. With flatbreads and a side dish of yoghurt, chick-peas, and preserved lemons. His mother would cook it on special occasions, which became rarer over time. He closed his eyes and visualised his mother squatting next to a small fire with the smell of wood burning and spitting meat fat. He remembered the glow of the fire, lighting up his mother's eyes while she gently rubbed oil and dried herbs into the flesh of the loin chops, then tossed them onto a white-hot metal grate. In the oven of bricks and mud the dough would gently rise, curling around the edges in a bowl shape, filling their shack with the most glorious aroma of baking bread. The sides of his mouth went giddy. Bread dipped in minty yoghurt and the zing of lemons. The meat then passed to him on a plastic plate by his mother while he devoured the crispy herb crust and darkened pink flesh with relish.

He shook his head back to his current reality: leading Isra, Mousa, and Mary with the goats to his side, into a ghostly town as the greenhouse feel of stifling air trapped within the clouds intensified and the ground became hotter on their ragged toes.

They meandered towards the town exhausted, caring little for their own safety. Isra noticed thin white squares on the ground, made of rusted metal. The squares were always noticeable around habitations, with a language she could not understand printed on the front. '*Communication tools,*' Mauricio had told her.

A giant sculpture, carved out of plaster sat above a crumbling, sinking building. Amiin peered at the sculpture, seeing a half-crescent moon and some kind of ball, about to topple out of the whitewash building.

"Islam was here, not so long ago," Mousa said.

Amiin stood transfixed at the pearly white building, now wilting in the sun. Islam. He had been told about the far-reaching powers of Islam, but the reality was he knew little about it; what it meant, and where it came from in the first place.

"Were you ever a convert?" Amiin asked.

Mousa shrugged. "I have met many folk who worshipped Allah, but not me."

Amiin looked at the cemented ball escaping from the building, wondering how long ago the worshippers had left this dusty mosque. The concrete huts were visible from a distance, uniformly white square shapes with frayed wooden roofs. The huts stood out from the landscape like beacons of a night. Amiin leant down and picked a flag off the floor as they approached the huts. It was navy blue with a faded white star in the middle. He placed it in his trouser pocket and pulled on the string attached to the goats.

Mousa chewed laconically on a dried chaat leaf. "Where are you taking us?"

Amiin turned around. The Haik around Mousa was hanging like a lop-sided sack to his body. His face appeared set back, like the flesh was sucking into the material. Amiin cleared his throat, spitting on the floor. "It's the nearest I see to water and food."

"What if our friends shooting the missiles hide here?" replied Mousa.

"I don't see any signs."

"How can you tell from here?"

"But how will we know unless we look."

Mousa coughed, as he spluttered, he felt his ribs. "I do not like this. We are safer amongst the elements."

"So, what do you suggest. Wandering further until we are mere skeletons brushing the ground?" Amiin replied, angrily.

Mousa turned to Mary. "We have done this for a long time, and we are still here, the two of us. We survived, so can you."

Amiin stared at Mousa exasperatingly. He spat on the floor again. "You fool."

"I see no fools here."

Amiin pointed at Mary. "You are deluded, you know that. Look at Mary's eyes, I see someone defeated. Someone beaten into submission by fanciful notions of freedom. Ha! Freedom! Freedom in your eyes is wandering with only rocks, sand and two goats for company."

Mousa fronted up to Amiin. Despite his meagre frame of flesh and bones his height dwarfed Amiin by inches. Amiin's eyes seethed with rage. He could smell acrid death rolling out of Mousa's lungs.

"You are the wise one are you, Amiin of the Coast? What are you but also a nomad. A stranger surviving day by day. Do not talk about her like that."

Amiin poked Mousa on the shoulder. "I was not offending Mary, just stating the obvious… see for yourself, you stupid doqonka!"

Mousa's countenance softened as he took a step away from Amiin. "Why don't you go back to your tiny town by the sea? This is our place. You are not made for the hinterland."

"Come with us or die out there. Your choice!" He brushed past Mousa. "Come, Ilhama."

Mousa threw the loose end of the Haik over his shoulder, threw the stick to the ground, and grabbed Mary by the shoulders. He shook her violently, jerking her body from side to side. She closed her eyes and pressed her lips together. "Amiin is right," she whispered morosely.

Mousa loosened his hands away from Mary's shoulders and took a step away. He looked away, disconsolate. In those couple of steps his body seemed to be much further than he was. "Fetch up the goats," he said, looking anxiously at the rows of concrete huts lining the road into the town.

"Mousa, you come with me. Isra and Mary can stay here with the goats. Once we have looked around to check it is safe you will get a signal from us."

"What kind of signal?" Isra replied.

"This…." Amiin cupped his hands around his mouth "Woo! Woo! Woo!" A sound like a wolf howling into the wind left his mouth. "Got that?"

Isra and Mary nodded.

"Why do I have to go. What about Mary?" Mousa asked.

"Isra will look after Mary. We won't be long, just a quick scout of the buildings."

"And what if SOMETHING is there?"

"Then we assess it and run the risk."

"Assess it? Ha!"

"Listen to Amiin, please," said Mary.

Mousa paced nonchalantly up to the goats. He touched the side of one of the goat's bodies, feeling the grainy texture of withering hair. A dull purple tongue was cradled up in the corner of its mouth, lifeless and cracked dry. He gave the goat dried grass from his hand, then quickly swung his stick in front, purposefully towards the town.

Amiin followed behind. "Remember the signal?" he shouted.

"Wolf howling badly. How could I forget?" Isra replied.

Amiin caught up to Mousa. "What is wrong with your leg?"

"Nothing is wrong. Why do you say?"

"Then why are you hobbling?"

"I slept on it awkwardly is all."

Amiin grabbed Mousa by the shoulder. He inspected Mousa's dogged, ragged disposition and his dirty Haik. The tang of his body odour had intensified, smelling like citrus. "Listen, my friend. I do not know what is hiding in there, chances are it could be nothing, but I need to know you've got my back. I am going in there for all of us. Remember that."

Mousa looked away from Amiin towards the outskirts of the town. He pulled Amiin's hands away from his shoulder. "Let us go then. FRIEND!" he said.

Plastic wrappers and bunches of smaller flags (in a similar pattern to the one Amin had picked up) flew in front of them as they approached the first concrete hut. Amiin looked behind where Isra and Mary sat behind a dying acacia tree. The goats were wandering around the tree, scavenging for scraps of leaves.

Sand flies dotted around his face, buzzing in and out of his hearing range. He approached the first hut, carefully placing one foot in front of the other. An image of his mother, teaching a boy how to walk on the beach appeared. He moved swiftly, around broken glass and piles of corroded metal pipes lying scattered on the ground. As he drew nearer to the entrance, he noticed mud nests nestled into the corner of the roof and flittering glimpses of swifts. The birds darted around the hut perimeter, like flies circling the tender flesh of exposed fruit. Mousa watched the birds from a distance. His face lightened, lifting his eyes out of the wormhole of the Haik and for the first time Amiin noticed a lightness of touch around the old goat-herder's features; smooth curving of the cheeks, milkiness around the forehead, a gentle sparkle from the iris.

The walls of the huts had a lime texture underneath the white paint. The shine on the walls had dimmed, reflective of the clouds. Mousa looked anxiously around, hesitantly ducking underneath the swift's flight, close to the tip of his nose.

Amiin pointed. "We'll go around the back."

A whistling wind engulfed the town, pinging from hut to hut like the rat-a-tat of a drum procession. Amiin tip-toed through the debris strewn on the ground. "Stick close to me. If I swing at anyone, back me up. You got that?"

Mousa nodded, focusing like a trance on the flight of the darting swifts. "Hear me?" Amiin repeated. Mousa snapped out of the daze sharply.

A metallic smell like tin burning on an open fire drifted out of the building. Amiin coughed, then led the way around the side of the east facing wall, kicking flags and broken glass out of the way as he circled around the perimeter. As he darted along the wall, he noticed pools of murky water giddying his eyes through a set of narrow grates in the basement. Mousa, clutching his stick, hung close to the threads of Amiin's shirt that waved in the hollow air. "I am here. Do not worry," Mousa whispered.

"What do you think is here?"

"One way to find out."

Amiin rushed ahead towards the back of the building. Mousa flung his knees forward but there was no way he could catch up with him. "Wait! Idiot boy, wait!" he shouted.

The back of the building was no more than a gigantic hole, without doors or windows. The shape of the frame looked lop-sided, as if an explosion had ripped the rear of the building into a mountain of concrete and pipes. Amiin walked up to a pile of papers strewn across the piles of concrete. He picked up a torn piece of paper:

MISSING FOR 6 MONTHS, 3 WEEKS, 1 DAY: ANY INFORMATION PLEASE CONTACT THE KIMASH

CENTRE. REWARD GRANTED FOR ANY WORTHWHILE INFORMATION

Underneath the font was a drawing of a girl's face, a young girl, with hair spiking in all directions like a wild cactus. Her disposition seemed confused, fearful. On either side of her eyes, high up in the temple, were blotchy marks reminiscent of desert dwellers where the sand and baking heat had punctured the skin.

"Think she's here?"

Amiin jumped and held his breath. "God almighty don't do that!"

"Do not run off then. Do you think these old legs can catch you in full sprint, boy?" Mousa tapped his knees with the stick. Amiin turned to the picture and caressed the paper. A shiver glided down his neck, for he felt helpless thinking about the lost girl, roaming the wastelands. He wiped the side of his face with the sleeve of his shirt.

"Toughen up, will you."

"HEY! HEY! ANYONE HERE?" Amiin screamed into the vacant field of air nestled between the two hut walls.

Amiin looked at Mousa dead in the eye with sneering contempt. For he knew Mousa was right — he had to toughen up. For every lost girl there was a breath of air, a heartbeat, a grain of rice that would keep him and Isra alive. He threw the pamphlet to the floor and rushed past him. "Come!" he yelled.

"Quiet, boy! We do not know who is in these buildings," Mousa whispered.

"What is the matter? Stop your moaning, old man, toughen up!"

"Xidhay!"

"Toughen up I say!" Amiin grinned innocuously at Mousa. The Haik was hanging lop-sided to his chest, exposing yellowing skin.

It gave Amiin a sudden boost, for he knew who was the stronger right now.

"AND WE ARE FREE SO SAY THE GOD THAT IS HE!" he yelled, throwing rocks at the building to their left.

"Stop it! NOW!" cried Mousa as he fumbled with the cloth around his face. A sweat-drop gathered on the tip of his nose.

"Why? There is nobody here. We are free, God said he. Is that right? I do not care."

Amiin, for the first in a long time let out a massive sigh of relief. A weight lifted from his shoulders; he could see it floating above the roofs of the buildings. He now did not mind acting the garish fool — in his heart he had always wanted to let the shackles off, just for a minute. But the burden of responsibility had always tied him down, like an anchor tied to the cornerstones of the desert.

"Have you turned into a madman? Ilaahay haku asturo!" Mousa shook his head, turned away from Amiin and marched to the front of the building.

"Where are you going?"

"To the others, foolish boy."

"Wait!"

Mousa turned around to face Amiin with a motionless expression. "To watch you alert the whole godforsaken town. I don't think so."

Amiin chased after Mousa. As he stomped through the rubble, he stepped on another pamphlet of the missing girl draped over two rocks. As his shoe collided with the rock the pamphlet ripped into two pieces. He picked up the pieces of paper and stuffed them into his trouser pocket.

A crack suddenly erupted out of the mountains of rubble to their right. It sounded like a mallet hammering into the face of a chalk hill; dusty, flat, devoid of echo. Amiin stopped suddenly, turned around to the nearest pile, and scanned through the broken glass and concrete slabs. Mousa stopped behind him. A dead silence ensued, stiller than the desert dawn. Amongst the rubble all movement ceased, it was like looking at a photograph — even the sand-flies disappeared.

Mousa's stick hung in the air, hanging like the branch of

a decaying tree. They both stayed rooted to the spot, Amiin covering his ears with his hands. He looked beyond the rubble at a blanket of dust that coated the background in a stolid wet-sand shade. He then lowered his hands, realising that they were completely helpless without weapons, naked to the elements. He watched a corner of the rubble, waiting for the inevitable — feeling a strange serenity. *A monster would pull itself out of the rubble, howling like a dog. The monster would look around dazed, shake its head which was large, as big as a giant boulder, then focus on the two of them cowering on the spot. Enormous eyes with tiny pupils would scan the surroundings.*

Mousa pulled a grimace and hung the stick above his head. The stick waved uncontrollably. Amiin awaited the monster.

A rustling ensued from the pile of rubble ahead. Out of the rubble a head appeared, a small head of little height. It was a young man, or a boy, he could not tell. He leapt to the floor behind a pile of rubble and signalled to Mousa to do the same. Mousa's knee quickly scraped against the floor as he dived behind an old post box. "Caddayn! Caddayn!" he whispered.

Amiin watched Mousa rolling around in agony. He threw his hands in the air. Mousa looked up. The Haik had flopped over his face as he lay still, silently clutching his knee.

A sandfly buzzed around Amiin, he flicked his hand at the fly and peered through the cracks of two breeze blocks. The boy approached, with a rifle slung over his shoulder. On his head, shielding half of his face was a grey cap, too large for his head. Amiin looked at his clothing; a grubby, oversized khaki uniform hung loosely from his frame and a pair of red sandals covered his feet.

The boy kicked stones on the ground, bobbling along the ground as if he were walking in a dream. Amiin looked beyond the boy but could see no one else. He then looked at Mousa, who was sitting up behind a jagged wall, watching the boy also. The hairs on the back of his neck bristled his skin. Hopefully *the boy will pass,* he thought. *Go away! Leave us! Go back to your dirty tribe or gang, or whatever it is*. Amiin nestled himself into a pile hole in the rubble where a large piece of concrete had cracked into two neat shapes. The concrete braised his arms as he wriggled into the small enclave — but he did not feel pain. His only feeling was pure terror about what would happen to Isra should the soldier find them.

The soldier kicked a stone at the slab Amiin was hiding behind. An echo of fear clanged through Amiin's chest. He lost sight of the soldier whose sandals slowly grazed along the road — slow, lumpy steps. Amiin curled his body into a ball and closed his eyes. His heartbeat raced and battered through his ribcage. He opened his eyes and peered carefully around the side of the slab to the road. The soldier had passed. He pressed his hands against the gravel and lifted his body delicately out of the hole. He could hear the crunching of foot moving slowly up the road, but the soldier was not there. He creeped up to the nearest wall to get a vantage point on Mousa.

The sandfly appeared again, this time flying around his shoes. He ignored the fly and bent around the wall. The soldier meandered up the road, kicking stones and picking up pieces of metal off the ground. He inspected the metal pieces finely, tucking one piece into the pocket of his loosely hung trousers. With his ragged hair sticking out of the cap and rudimentary walking style, Amiin saw for the first time not a soldier, or even an enemy. He saw a naked embryo, a new-born cub — baking in the vicious, sprawling emperor of the land, the mighty sun hiding behind a guard of clouds.

The soldier was within ten feet of the wall where Mousa was hiding. He suddenly panicked, predicting the next act. He picked a rock up off the floor and was about to throw it away from the wall when a sudden fall suddenly caught his eye, inviting him to re-focus.

It was the soldier, collapsing like a sack of corn to the ground. Mousa's body appeared from behind the soldier holding a sharp, bloody rock in his right hand. Amiin looked on, disbelieving, as Mousa hammered the next blow into the face of the soldier while the body squirmed on the floor.

The whole event took hours. Even the blows, which pulverised the boy's skull into the floor; four, five, six before Amiin could move his feet and stop Mousa landing any more blows.

Amiin approached the scene; with an icy stream of blood-flow gushing through his neck. Mousa's hands were shaking uncontrollably. He turned and looked at Amiin, then pulled back the Haik from his face. Revealed was a countenance of surprising serenity. His chin tucked in neatly and a moist glaze covered his eyes. "What did you do, you old fool?" Amiin said mournfully. "WHAT DID YOU DO!"

The boy, the soldier, lay on the ground. His body now open to all the elements that the sun could bring.

Chapter Five

Mousa's panting greeted the goats. The goats, looking sprightly, immediately stood up. He patted one of the goats on the head, then turned towards Mary curled up in a ball, in a ditch beyond a stone wall. He threw the stick to the ground.

"What did you find?" she said, hopefully.

Mousa stroked the sides of Mary's hair. "An enemy."

"An enemy… what happened?"

He turned the cloth away from his face, biting his bottom lip. "It does not matter. We cannot go back there."

"But why?"

A flash quickly enveloped around Mousa's eyes. "We must go, untie the goats." Amiin then suddenly jumped over the wall.

"Do as I say. Untie the goats and stay with Isra."

She coughed. "Did you find any water or food?"

Mousa turned around with venomous eyes, picked the stick off the floor, and thrashed it towards Mary. The butt licked Mary on the ear. She stumbled, coughing. Her hopeless expression turned solemnly into submission. She felt her ear. Blood was leaking from the side of her lobe onto the ground. She immediately ran to the goats.

"Old fool! What is wrong with you, eh?" Amiin shouted. He tugged at Mary's dress and brought her body closer. "Let me see" he said, pulling the side of her head closer.

Mousa gathered the goats, muttering profanities under his breath.

Amiin inspected the delicate child cradled in his arms. Her skin was milky and cold. He could feel a jittery pulse and fear oozing out of her lungs, about to spill onto the ground. "Hold your head still," he said and pulled her hair gently back from behind the bloody ear. "Sssh... it's okay."

A fiery red bruise was expanding around the ear, like a tumor. The blood dripped along her shoulder, down her arm and onto the ground. The cut was not particularly long, but deep into the tissue.

Her head twitched to the side. "I must sit," she said.

"We cannot mend it now, we must move. She will live — but not for long if we stay here…" Mousa announced. "… NOW!"

Amiin glared at Mousa. The two sets of eyes met head on, like two pythons circling the ground. Amiin looked deep, as far as he could go into the dark matter of Mousa's eyes. It was a blotchy, greying darkness, like how he imagined the bottom of the sea. *What lives at the bottom of the sea?* he thought. He had heard tales of deformed fish and crustaceans with heads fifty times the size of their bodies and of shape-shifting centipedes and jellyfish as large as whales. Only the strongest evolved at the bottom of the ocean; and Mousa was incarcerated in his own prison of the desert. Mousa was not scared, nor had he thought for a second about killing a boy, for it was the most primeval survival instinct that he possessed; to his being and the others around him.

Amiin knew he was right for now, they had to move. Many more of the soldiers would arrive and they needed water, food, shelter, just like they did.

He picked a piece of green cloth off the ground, shook it, and held it tightly against Mary's ear. "Hold this," he said, placing her left hand against the pressed cloth. Her arm melted in the palm of his hand, limp and lifeless. He looked into her forlorn face; her eyes were glazed, and saliva was creeping out of the side of her mouth. He then hauled her body onto his shoulder and signalled to Isra.

Isra stood up from the stone wall. "What happened? There is blood all over your shirt." She glared at Mousa.

"Nothing we cannot sort out. Grab the bags and the sheet. We must go. NOW!"

Isra gasped at the flatlined body of Mary, hanging off Amiin's shoulders like a dried piece of meat. "Is she okay?"

"Dazed is all." Amiin glared at Mousa. "We move back into the desert — east towards the Horn."

"The Horn? What will we do there except die of thirst?" Isra protested.

The goat bells chimed in the wind. Mousa turned towards the town, the scene of the crime. For a second Amiin thought he saw a glimpse of emotion.

He dipped his shoulder where Mary hung and placed her on the ground and held her face close. "We have no choice. They are coming, Ilhama." He pointed at an area of the rocky hills on the other side of the town. "Do you see that?"

"What am I looking at?" Isra replied.

Rugged red contours buried into the cliffs, making the rocks look like steps. "THAT!" Amiin moved Isra's shoulders towards the incline where a trail of smoke drifted.

"The cliff-face?"

"The smoke plume, look with your eyes!" he shouted.

Isra squinted at the rocky cliff, past the edge of town. She rolled her tongue in the inside of her mouth. "It could be a dust cloud… residue heat… anything."

"Residue heat?"

"From the sunrays or something."

"Ilhama that is smoke from an explosion, did you not hear it?"

Isra's expression drifted into panic, her eyes bulging. "What... whhhaaaat do you mean? Is it the bandits with the wild hyenas? The ghosts from the sea?"

Amiin suddenly felt an urge to hold Isra tight. He grabbed her by the shoulders and flung her arms around his waist. Her grip was loose, and he could feel the flesh that had withered around his hips. He kissed the top of her scalp covered in dust. Her hair was thinning at the crown, un-matting her once dark, lustrous locks into fine pieces of thread that blew softly into the wind.

"It was a soldier."

"A soldier?"

"Yes, a soldier. Remember I told you."

"The bandits with nasty weapons?"

"Something like that."

Isra pulled away from Amiin, looking him in the eye. "What happened back there?"

He looked away, tilting his head towards the goats and Mousa. He then turned to the purple iridescent trickle on Mary's neck. She was sitting up, using all her strength to keep the cloth to her ear.

"Ilhama, we do not have time. Help me," he pleaded.

Amiin lifted Mary back onto his shoulders while Isra stared distantly at the town and the ever-decreasing plume of smoke. *It signified something. Some unimaginable horror,* she thought.

"Where will we take her?" Isra asked.

"I don't need anything, I'm just fine," said Mary.

Amiin turned to Isra. "She needs a clean dressing, stitches. But we cannot go back there."

Isra turned to the wasteland beyond the town southbound, a sprawling yellow sheet glistening like a patchwork of marble against the ever-increasing light nestling up to the clouds. She scrambled together the possessions that were left on the floor into the rucksack; a tarpaulin cover, some corn husks, two tins of beans, a pashmina jumper, a bundle of cotton rags, two tin plates, a porcelain mug, bundle of sticks, a reel of frayed rope and a plastic Geri-can.

Amiin suddenly fell to the floor clutching his knees, vomiting. "Brother! What is wrong?" She dropped the bag and knelt next to him.

Amiin signalled to her with the index finger of his left hand to where Mousa was heading. The colour of his face was lightening with pink dots engulfing his cheeks. She glanced at his arms resembling the wings of a locust hugging the floor.

She then felt a depth of despair in the pit of her stomach. It reminded her of something vividly. The last plague, three years ago:

A*ppearing on the horizon like a storm cloud. She was*

caught in the tornado of locusts hopping all over her body, thousands, millions. Vying for a dusty piece of crop to eat. The wall of chirping shrieks! That was the only time she failed to hear Amiin screaming to get in under the cover. The same tarpaulin sheet she had just stowed away.

Despite the noise and shape shifting patterns of the swarm they were harmless to her; she did not mind them. The tales she had heard from the village folk were another story; fields of wheat decimated within hours and of rivers quenched dry. Of killer locusts among the swarm, who preyed on human blood and could drink a whole human body within ten minutes.

On one such occasion a family lived in a small dwelling on the outskirts of Quardho: father, mother, grandmother, and child. They had locked all their doors and taped hessian bags around broken windows to repel the swarm.

As the family heard the buzzing shriek they hid under a table, waiting for the swarm to pass. But the swarm was ravaging, insatiable. The swarm found gaps in the brickwork and managed to move a hessian bag to create an opening in the building. Neighbours gasped in horror as the swarm piled into the house, creating a black space within, like a dead night that had nowhere to go but up; into the bedroom, toilet, into the attic and out the back, devouring the pepper and tomato plants and the little patch of brown grass gasping in the sun. Kicking over tables, chairs, toys. Even a small car.

When the swarm eventually passed all that was left was a sea of droppings and four corpses, lying curled up in tight balls close to one another. The screams unheard by neighbours, drowned out by the drone of millions of locusts purring in delight, with bellies full.

She helped Amiin to his feet, looking down at the vomit strewn on a dried piece of grass. He gasped for the dry air, wiping his mouth with a sleeve, all the while facing the ground like a man condemned.

"Where is the goat herder?" he said, gasping.

"Ahead, not far. With the goats."

"Wher—' he coughed violently. "Wheeeeere?"

"Not far, brother."

He turned towards Mary, reluctantly nodding, his head flopping sideways. "Call him."

Isra propped his head up and wiped his mouth with a rag. "We neeeeed him," he slurred.

Isra then felt a burst of energy through her thighs. She leapt off the ground and ran, dodging boulders and ditches in the ground until she reached the stone wall. She leapt, free as a gazelle, over the wall. Her bare feet landed on a sharp stone that cut her left sole. She continued regardless, up the hill that led into the wilderness.

"Mousa! Hey!" She waved her hands frantically, gasping for air. One of the goats turned around, chewing on a lip. Mousa loosened the rope harness and stopped. His head was covered, giving off the impression of a spirit drifting along the rocks. "What little one?" he said.

She cautiously approached. "Mary is not well, neither is my brother. We need your help."

Mousa lifted the hood and turned around. The goats also turned; their eyes glued to their master. "Stupid girl. Questioning me!" he muttered. "I have not left her for half a kilometre, and she needs me. Ha!"

"What was that?" Isra replied.

His eyes gleamed a faint rogue "She needs me now, doesn't she? That will teach her" he spat on the ground.

Isra bit her tongue. "Yes, she needs you. We need you."

"And what of your brother?"

"He said to call you. We are being chased."

He spat again and pulled the harness tight. The goats jolted, like they were pulling to attention "What if we are?"

"We cannot manage. Mary is bleeding heavily, and Amiin is sick" she said, trying to hide the panic in her voice.

"Sick? Weak boy. What is wrong with him?"

"He's exhausted and may have something wrong from the inside."

He nodded, stroking the hair on his chin. "I was coming

back for Mary. You do know that don't you? I was just teaching her a lesson. Obey your master."

A tear slid down Isra's cheek. She looked down at the hill where the two crumpled bodies were flayed out like thin slices of meat. "Please help us," she said quietly.

"And what do I get in return? Our alliance was severed in the town by your stupid brother. Why should I help him now?" He looked luringly at Isra, from the waist down.

Isra had seen the way Mousa would look at her. Different to how Amiin or Mary saw her. His tongue would roll around his cracked mouth and his eyebrows would sink right on top of his eyes. If this was desire, then she had seen it time after time. She had heard stories about sex and prostitution and about how it was the oldest profession, going back to Ancient Egypt. Feeling desperation, she felt there was no other way so lifted her dress off the floor and revealed her bronzed legs to Mousa. She looked away ashamed, knowing Amiin would detest her actions. What she was offering was still unclear, for she was only just starting to bleed into a ripe virgin, but she had seen it done before by girls on the beach when they were desperate for provisions.

Isra's interaction with men had always been minimal, nothing more than idle chat while Amiin was by her side. She had only seen a penis when Amiin was getting changed, a fleeting glimpse she had little curiosity with. *How would it fit? And how would it become hard when it was soft and limp? Would it hurt?* Her desire to help her brother knew no bounds. She focused on Amiin.

"So, you are offering yourself to me, girl?"

She took a deep breath, nodding reluctantly. "Only when we are safe."

He tugged the rope. "Okay, little flower, it shall be. But no complaining to your brother once I help him off the floor — this is a deal."

"Yes, this is a deal. We must go, we do not have much time!"

Mousa wiggled a finger to Isra, beckoning her towards him. "Uh uh! A kiss to seal the deal or I stay here."

She looked down the hill, then turned to Mousa, dragging her feet in the gravel. A strange smell surrounded Mousa, like lemons wilting in the heat. His body grew inch by inch, darkening around her as her body glided into the dirty Haik. He threw his stick to the ground and embraced her. Her body stuck to the Haik. That putrid smell again.

He leant down and looked Isra dead in the eye. His breath had that familiar tang to it. She noticed blood lines, swimming through the whites of his eyes and long hairs shooting out of his nose. She then closed her eyes and fell headfirst towards his pink, cracked lips. Tasteless, except tiny pieces of gritty skin. Mousa grabbed her behind and pulled her closer. They were locked together, staring at the world. Chance had brought them together and chance had saved them. As she pulled away, he grabbed her arm.

She shed a tear, then brushed the teardrop from her cheek to the ground. The last tear of innocence evaporating into the desert.

Chapter Six

Isra lay awake, the moon shining in full glow like an act of defiance against the clouds. She stared at it, picking out shades on the surface she had not seen before.

She had agreed to meet Mousa when the moon was highest in the sky, behind a row of bushes where they had camped for the night. Mary's wound was healing, and Amiin's lethargy was passing as they laid in their sleeping bags blissfully unaware of a seedy exchange about to commence.

The outline of Mousa's Haik resembled a giant crow as she slithered gently towards the man about to break her virginity. It lasted a long time, or so it felt.

She lay on the ground, naked to the elements while Mousa scraped his bristly chin on her face, grunting like a pig. The Haik dwarfed her, wrapping tight the two bodies. Her skin shone luminant against the moonlight, lighting up the ground in the moments when Mousa's winged shadow took a rest.

He puffed and wheezed, taking regular sips of a water bottle, for his stamina was not what it used to be. Isra looked away the whole time from Mousa's deranged, lustful expression. The only point she could focus on was an acacia tree to her right. She stared intently at the weeping branches in the moonlight brushing the ground and the trunk leaning to one side, like it was near death.

Her vagina hurt, a scraping sensation.

She bit her bottom lip as Mousa kissed her body, spraying a vapor of sinewy guts into her nose. He attempted to kiss her lips, but she turned the other way, praying that the ordeal would be over soon. *Was this rape?* She bit her lip again. Her legs shivered, dry.

Mousa continued to thrust her body into the ground. He suddenly jerked and stopped. A drop trickling out of her genitals. She quickly pushed his body away; thankful it was over. He had promised not to ejaculate inside her, and for that she was irked. But for now, she just wanted the comfort of her tent, and to lie next to her brother.

His knees creaked as he got to his feet and pulled the Haik around his waist.

She sat cross-legged, with her back facing Mousa. "Are we done?" she hushed into the pearly night.

He smirked. "Whatever you think, child."

She closed her eyes, trying to divert her mind elsewhere… anywhere… until she reached her father.

Was he tall, like Amiin? Did he have a thick scalp of wiry hair? Did he chew food loudly? And what of his family? And the generation before? And before? Never had she thought about the man who had one day planted a seed in her mother's belly, then disappeared into the night like a ring of smoke at a campfire.

She quickly leapt off the ground and sprinted towards the tent. Her vagina was sore, hindering the movement of her legs. She arrived just short of the tent and looked down at her cotton trousers where blood spots had appeared around the crotch area. She quickly took them off, exposing her raw flesh to the moon. The temperature suddenly dipped, rattling the marrow of her bones. She tossed the trousers inside the tent, creeping inside deftly.

That night she lay awake, in a state of bewilderment. She was sore in places she had not been before. A voice in her head echoed, *"Calm down, forget it. In this world we often must do things we do not particularly want to do. But we must think of our survival, and our family, Isra; for there is nothing more important. If you had lost Amiin back at the town, you would not be far behind. He is here now, resting and recuperating, when he could have been a prisoner for the bandit army or carrion for the vultures... Do not forget that!"*

She closed her eyes, throwing the image of the big crow smothering her body to the back of her mind.

Amiin awoke in the morning with an injection of colour

to his face. Isra was by his side, patting a wet cloth on his forehead. She looked down at the barred flesh of Amiin's milky white legs; at shin bones tearing through the flimsy sheen of skin, purple dots scattered around the thighs, matchstick toes quivering uncontrollably. His eyes flickered, hiding from the light.

"Making us worry, brother."

Amiin looked around the tent, shock flushing through his eyes. He gripped the fabric of the sleeping bag tightly. "Where... where are we?"

"South of the last place. Cannot remember the name. Not too far."

"Why... why... arrrrrre we here?"

She pulled the cloth away from his forehead. "You had checked out on us. Thought we would rest here until you recovered."

"Who is we?"

"Mousa, Mary. And the goats."

Amiin stretched his legs and shot his neck forward, holding his stomach and grimacing. "How long… how long have we been here, Ilhama?"

"Few days."

Amiin inspected Isra's expression, one of relief and pain. Her face had a copper sheen, different to how he remembered. Her lips were puffy and purple, her hair longer and wild like a tangled mesh of prickly bushes. "You were out cold, brother, some kind of blood infection the wise man said."

"The wise man?"

"Yes. The wise man. We met him outside of the town. He looked like a shepherd, or a missionary I am not sure…" She held his forehead with the outside of her palm. "We owe him, otherwise you would be dead. He gave you a special kind of milk from a plant, but you are here. Oh, you are here brother… I'm so pleased you are here!" She squeezed Amiin so tightly he coughed. His feeble grip tapped Isra on the shoulder. He wanted to hold his sister but had little strength. She pulled away.

"Where is the wise man now?"

"He was going south, Zanzibar Island he said."

Amiin smirked. "And what did he look like?"

"He wore robes, and had a long mane of dark, greying hair. His skin was soft for an old man and his smile was kind."

Amiin shook his head, disbelieving. "You could not make this up, Ilhama."

"Make what up?"

He wiped the sweat off his forehead with the palm of his hand. He looked at the outside of his palm curiously. The shadowy green tributaries, pulsing out of the thin flesh. Red dashes, peppered across his knuckles, fingernails as yellow as the sands. "It doesn't matter."

Isra turned away, a tear trickling down her cheek. She packed a tin-pot into a rucksack, then took her jumper off and stuffed it in. It was then she suddenly noticed a certain brightness lighting up the interior of the tent. A dull lightness, but enough to cast small shadows from the outside. She checked the flashlight on the floor. It was turned off.

She felt a warmness. The heat was running up her arms into her shoulders and through her ears. "Does it seem lighter to you?" she said, touching the canvas.

"A little…" He lay back on the ground, burying his head in the sleeping bag. "…I have been out for days."

She crawled to the entrance and unzipped the fabric. A sharp blue hue stung her pupils, making her body swing to the side in an unnatural motion. She covered her eyes, then slowly released her fingers until the sky was within sight. Clouds were in the sky, defiant to their blue master about to swallow them whole. Then the sun appeared, burning bright in the east. Isra shielded her eyes again. The sky shimmered and glistened to the tone of the sun as if the star conducted an orchestra that lit the desert up like a red room.

She opened her eyes and stumbled out of the tent, beaming up at the beautiful blue before her very eyes, more beautiful than any ocean, sea, or river. A perfect azure blue: the colour that had haunted her dreams and teased her through holes in the clouds, offering glimpses of the atmosphere beyond; the ionosphere, the edge of the earth, stars, galaxies.

Amiin had told her about the other worlds, which were like pinpricks of light billions upon trillions of miles away. Worlds that also rotated around a star where life could exist, but we would never know. He told her about man's failed quest to find life among the stars hundreds of years ago, when money and resources were plentiful. The end of the prosperous time. *Another prophetic tale from Mauricio, no doubt,* she thought.

The few clouds that remained brightened against the blue backdrop, shapeshifting from a lion's face to husks of wheat, vulture's beak to bearded man, pointing directly at her. It was like sinking her mind back through time, right back to a time when humans had not even hatched from the shell. If this was heaven, she wanted to float up right now, away from the toil on the ground.

Amiin poked out of the tent flap. "Well good morning, beautiful blue. I have missed you!" He slumped down on the canvas, gazing in awe at the sky. "See, I told you it would make an appearance again."

They both closed their eyes, listening to the faint purr of a breeze brushing by.

She exhaled slowly through her nose: "Do you remember the ant game? What was it called?"

"La corsa dei nostri tempi!" he replied.

"La corsa dei…"

"Nostri tempi"

"What does it mean, brother?"

"I think it translated to the race of our times, something like that."

Isra's eyes blushed. She hid her hands underneath her backside. "Did you ever win?"

"Why do you ask? Have you seen a colony?"

"Of ants?"

Amiin nodded.

"Not seen them for weeks, used to always be crawling into my shoes. Annoying trivial things."

Ammin grimaced. His hands shielded his tender stomach. "To answer your question, I did win once. Not a hefty sum. Couple of coppers to trade for water."

"Is that all?"

"Mauricio always wanted to play. He would get this twinkle in his eye when he thought a thoroughbred was crawling through his fingers." He smiled, looking beyond the flap of the tent to the naked sky.

"Like a wild stallion running the ground… This! He would proclaim. This is authentic. Look at the colour, the right shade of blood red along the spine. And the legs are longer than the darker ones. These are the stronger, quicker, more resolute ones, Amiin. I will bet you five coppers! And he would set the race off without delay."

He shuffled closer to Isra, feeling the breeze massage the tip of his nose. "The colour of the skin, the legs, the warped vision of a super-ant — it was all a big guess. For old Mau it was all about the whim, like he could smell good luck in the air or something."

Isra zipped her jacket up. "And was he a success?"

He laughed. "Ouch!" he giggled, clutching his stomach. "Ouch!"

"What is so funny?"

He pushed the sleeping bag away from the dampened skin. The smile faded, into the recess of sandy cheeks. "The old man who treated me. What was he wearing?"

"Rags of cloth tied together, a make-shift Salwar Kameez, sandals. Don't remember a lot else."

"Not exactly the finest silk, were they?"

"What does that mean?"

"The betting caught up with him. Debts! The curse of man."

He had not touched her hair since before his collapse. The days had made the texture feel smoother, like a pebble on the shore. Her head felt warmer.

"Was he a bad person? For you know… betting on the ants?"

"No, no, he was not a bad person. It is easy to get into debts when you do not have two sticks to rub together, Ilhama. Mauricio was just trying to survive, hustle a copper here and there. It is easy to get involved with the wrong people. Mau was the same."

"How much did he owe?"

"I do not know, but I do not think it was much. Knowing Mau, it was probably a bet on those stupid ants or a historical fact about the Babylonians or something."

"But if he was borrowing coppers to eat that can't be bad, can it."

"Never saw him eat a crust."

For a second she peered deep into the heart of the sun. At coronal white streams that were painful on the retinas, then orange specks that flooded her vision. She turned away quickly, gasping.

"What is wrong, Ilhama?"

Isra giggled, into the heart of the sun. Her eyes remained sealed shut, slowly opening into the heart of her brother. He peered back at her, a glint appearing in the corner of his eye.

She turned to the ocean in the sky, away from the sun. *Mauricio… It was you, wasn't it!*

Chapter Seven

A cacophony of noise erupted outside of their tent the following morning; tin pots clanging together, goats yawning, then a scream.

Amiin lifted the tent flap and peered outside. He could see Mousa yelling expletives at Mary, who was sitting cross-legged outside of their tent. Mousa's arms flayed wildly against the backdrop of the blue sky while the goats timidly kept their distance, sniffing the ground for further signs of danger.

Amiin turned to Mary's withdrawn countenance facing the ground. It was the first time he had caught sight of Mary since rising into consciousness. She appeared older, a harder outline of her face, blushed skin, thinner hair. If he looked closely her lips were chewing on her tongue. Mousa picked up a tin can and smashed it on the floor, in front of Mary.

"See what they are doing," said Amiin.

Isra closed the tent flap. "Their arguments are nothing new."

Amin picked an apple core off the ground. "Arguments?" He chewed it slowly.

"Yes, arguments, brother. Arguments. Hardly an easy relationship is it."

"I do not remember arguments. Mousa being a bully yes, but Mary would not argue back."

Isra sighed. "He has not been kind to her for days."

"Kind? He hit her over the head with a stick!"

"He acted like he cared when the wound was gushing blood onto the ground. He even apologised to her. But it soon healed, and Mary was being shouted at again. Said it was her fault."

"What was her fault?"

"The bash around the head."

Amiin's face turned red. He threw the sleeping bag to one side and wriggled his feet out of the tent flap. "I will give him a headache, the bastard xoogsheegasho!"

She grabbed him by the shoulder. "What are you doing?"

He wiped his brow. "What does it look like? I want to give that shit sucking bastard a piece of my mind!" he gasped for air. "Let me go, Ilhama."

"Look at you. You can barely walk." She tugged at Amiin's shoulder, pushing him away from the flap. He wheezed and gasped, before lying down onto a sweaty cushion.

"This is not right! I saw what he did. Saw it with my own eyes… xoogsheegasho!"

"What do you mean?"

A fly flew in through the flap, hovering over Isra's head and landed onto her forehead. He glanced at the fly before Isra swiped it away. He then nudged towards her. "I was going to keep quiet about it, but there is something you should know about our friend over there."

"Who, Mousa?"

"Yes."

"Well?"

"Well, he… he killed somebody."

Isra's eyes jittered from side to side. Her hand grabbed the sleeping bag tightly. "Who did he kill?"

Amiin wiped his eyes. He was hoping the long sleep and the incident in the town had all been a dream; a long winding tale where he was falling off the end of the world into the darkest abyss only to be woken up and told he was alive and well. This was the moment he had been dreading. He gripped her shaking hands into his milky palm.

"It was back in the town, a boy soldier."

Terror blazed through the whites of Isra's eyes. "Why? Were you in trouble?"

"We could have escaped. The boy had not seen us."

"Who was he fighting for?"

"I do not know. It looked like a ragtag army of sorts. They

are the ones firing the mi—" he stopped abruptly, pulling his teeth together.

"Firing?"

"Is that what I said?"

"Firing, you said firing."

"Oh, I meant the horns we sometimes hear in the distance, when it is late."

"What about them?"

Amiin widened his lips and looked Isra in the eye. "This bunch of bandits could be the ones firing their horns into the air. To let us know they are coming."

Isra turned to the side. The fly reappeared, this time on her cheek. "It was always the jackals, or the hyenas, or wild dogs…" She slapped her hand on her cheek, squashing the fly. "… and you agreed with me."

A faint tingling of bells came from outside. Isra opened the flap to see one of the goats sniffing the ground. Mousa was breaking down the tent hurriedly while Mary gathered sticks, tying them into tight bundles with a ball of string.

"What is it?" Amiin asked.

Isra wrapped a shoal around her face "Let me see." Amiin grabbed her by the arm. His grip quickly weakened as she pushed away out of the tent flap.

"What is going on?" she asked Mary.

Mary turned to face Isra deftly, like a cat facing its prey. Isra noticed a deftness of touch as she wrapped the sticks in neat bundles then threw them to the floor. Her wound had nearly healed, and her face seemed fuller, with a vibrancy of colour around the jowls. "You scared me," she said.

"Sorry, what are you doing?"

"Packing up"

"You are leaving?"

"Sorry, Isra, I was about to wake you. The time has come to leave." Mary nodded towards the great red corridor to the west. To the very path they had toiled for days where the unhindered sun rays beat down amongst dripping orange clouds.

"I'm looking at what?" Isra asked.

Mary pointed at the tip of a brilliant white cloud drifting eastwards. "Don't you see? It is one of the missiles."

Isra tripped over a peg in the ground and ran towards the tent, noticing Mousa's eyes poking out of the Haik from behind a wall. He signalled to Mary to untie the goats. Then a crashing noise echoed from beyond the western horizon where a jagged array of rocky hills ascended out of the town. It crashed again, rippling through the rocks. Another crash, this time sounding far closer. Amiin poked his head out of the tent and gingerly stood up.

He hobbled towards Isra and Mary. "Where did it come from?" he asked.

Isra pointed to the spot where the plumes of smoke were rising into the clouds. Amiin shielded his eyes and looked to the rocky western road, beyond the town of death. Despite the commotion it was eerily silent. He then shoved a hand into a side pocket of his trousers for the binoculars.

"Where did you find those?" Isra asked.

"Weeks ago, forgot I had them," he replied.

"Rocks!" she laughed, pointing to rock and sand, sand, and rock. The dry waste.

He slowly lifted the binoculars and curled his eyelids around the viewing glasses. With the tips of his fingers, he adjusted the lens and waited.

"What is it? What is it?" Isra shouted impatiently.

"Tell us, Amiin!" said Mary. Mousa stood still by the wall, with arms crossed.

Amiin's body stood perfectly still, leaning onto his left leg. He tightened his grip around the binoculars.

"Well?" Mousa said.

The binoculars slipped from his grasp. His eyes fixed onto the rocky corridor in a trancelike state, pupils dilated with eyebrows pushed high into the brow.

"We have to go now!" he said.

"Let me see that!" Mousa leaped over the wall and shoved Amiin in the back. The binoculars fell to the ground.

Mousa swiped at them like an aggressive lion. He lifted the binoculars into his eyes with the lens pointing inwards.

Isra looked at Mary, they both giggled. "Shut your mouth, stupid girls," he said, turning the lens towards the west.

"In agreement then?" said Amiin.

Mousa held onto the binoculars. "They don't look far," he said, non-plussed.

"Who's they?" Isra asked. "Tell me!"

The goats gravitated towards Mousa, sniffing his feet like scavenger dogs. "I can see about twenty of them, clad loosely in khaki. The monkeys!"

"Soldiers?" said Mary.

Mousa chewed the bottom of his lip. "Appears so."

"Do they have weapons?" Isra asked.

"Can't see it…" Mousa spat red on the floor, keeping the binoculars tight to the lip of his eye. "… some kind of rocket launcher is making all that smoke."

"Run!" shouted Amiin. "Run, everyone. They have caught up with us thanks to this goat-eating bastard!"

Mousa threw the binoculars to the floor, looking at Amiin sternly. "I never eat my goats. How dare you!"

"Listen, you idiot, they are less than a mile away, heading down the hill straight for us." The crack of another explosion ran down the hill exploding to the right of their camp. The propulsion of noise hit Amiin straight in the sinuses. He leaned over, rubbing the back of his head. Mousa grabbed the goats with the rope.

"What do we do?" said Isra.

"I cannot go far, Ilhama." He glanced into her eyes feeling helpless again. "Go! Just go with the others. I will hide out here. They may not even see me."

"What do they want?"

"Mousa, that is why you must go. Take this…." He pulled a dusty flare out of the tent. "When the sun rises, fire this into the sky and I will come and find you." From another pocket a small clock appeared. Isra looked at it briefly. It had a leather strap with numbers circling the clock face. "Take this also."

"But that could be miles, and what if we move? How do I fire it?"

A calmness cloaked Amiin's face. He pointed to a cord at the back of the flare "Release this once you have pointed it into the sky and pull hard. Make sure you stay well back. Listen, you must persuade Mousa to stay in the same spot for a few hours. Okay?"

Isra's eyes dropped. She just wanted to nurse her brother back to health.

"Just go, I will catch you up in the early hours. Remember the time?" He pointed to the wristwatch.

"Four."

"Then what are you waiting for? They will be passing soon. GO! GO, I SAID!" He pushed Isra away. And with the push he knew he was pushing her back into the wilderness. The sweepstake of life or death splayed out across the horizon as the clouds gathered.

She looked at Amiin, then dropped her head to the ground and begrudgingly followed Mousa and Mary up the hill.

Amiin bit his bottom lip as Isra's body moved slowly away from his.

A burning sulphureous smell clung to the dry air. He took a deep breath, his stomach felt tight; a sudden sense of loss scavenged his insides. A sharp feeling that burned his ribs and quelled the hunger pains. He took another breath and with all the energy he could muster hobbled over to the tent and pulled the pegs out of the red earth. His legs felt like a log was tied to them and his breath was shallow. He threw the pegs on the ground and released the exterior sheets from the tent poles. The tent was dismantled and stowed away in a rucksack within minutes. He dragged the rucksack along the floor, gasping for air. A water can had been left behind. He lifted the can but was unable to tip the water into his mouth so leant down and poured the water carefully into his hands and gulped voraciously.

Over the wall he saw a Geed Hindi tree laying on its side. The leaves of the tree were changing from supple green to a whitened shade of orange. He then stood up as the insufferable weight of the rucksack bared down on his shoulder. He shuffled up to the wall, threw the rucksack over and grabbed at the wall-rocks until his body was over and lying back down in the sandy earth, underneath the tree.

He looked up at the growing mass of clouds now covering the sun while a scuttling of footsteps reverberated. He shuffled onto his belly until he was hidden within the entanglement of branches and dying leaves. Stars appeared amongst the branches, outlines of an oasis and what seemed like Isra to his right. Closing his eyes he hugged the rucksack and stared at another blue spot developing in the clouds. Then a cold tip pressed against his cheek. He swatted it away as his eyelids drew. The tip dug further into his cheek, feeling warmer. The smell grew in intensity. He coughed, opening his eyes to a khaki uniform bearing down on his body as the world around him turned black.

Chapter Eight

The endless carpet of red land appeared before Isra, wider and more engulfing than before as she scratched at the parched ground with a stick.

She looked up at the light spot in the clouds where the sun hid, wondering when she would see the beautiful blue sky again, and Amiin. As she tilted her head away from the lightened speck, she titled towards the grey blanket hanging ominously in the sky. The clouds and the desert looked like one big bowl, with the white froth of the clouds on top and the dry bed trickling away at the bottom. The grey middle floating on forever.

Mary crouched down to the goats. "You have recovered well. Considering," said Isra.

Mary stroked one of the goats behind the ear. "Considering what, Isra?"

"So many things… lack of water, food, the sweltering heat." Isra pointed to Mousa drifting sideways as he wandered in the near distance.

"Didn't have much choice, did I?" Mary replied, pensively. "You too are a child of these surroundings, Isra. You have to put up with what I do. But we must carry on regardless… right?"

Isra put her rucksack on the ground. "Here," she hushed.

"What is it?"

"I'll show you."

Out of the bag came a tin can. Isra pulled the ring-pull off. "Ssh"

Inside the tin were slices of peaches, swimming in syrup. "Oh my!" Mary gasped. "Where did you find this?"

Isra dipped a finger into the syrup with her finger. "Found it," she said.

Mary looked down into the pink dashes running through the gloopy liquid. The peaches shone like pearls on a beach drenched in moonlight. "How old is it?"

Isra turned the tin to one side. "Does not say. Don't they keep forever in tins?"

Mary beamed from ear to ear. "It is beautiful."

"Try one," said Isra.

"What does it taste like?"

"Like bliss… swimming in sweet water."

Mary stepped away from Isra. "Cannot remember the last time I had fruit. Mousa says it will make my teeth fall out."

"Tuh! And corn will make your ears drop-off."

"Could it?"

"Of course it will not! Try one. I promise your teeth will not fall out."

Mary looked around. Mousa was squatting with his back turned.

"Before I change my mind!"

Mary put two fingers into the tin and grasped at a slice of peach. She clawed one away from the syrup and scooped it carefully out of the tin. The slice then squirmed out of her grasp and landed on the ground. She dived at the slice instinctively and scooped it into her fingers, blew the grit away and threw it into her mouth.

"That was impressive. A wild cat could not have pounced on that quicker!"

The look of wonder dissipated from Mary's face as she closed her eyes. Isra could see her face slowly dissolving into a riot of colour and textures; her lips quivered, shoulders dipped. For a moment Isra could see Mary, the girl free of shackles.

"Not bad, is it?"

Mary rolled the peach around her mouth, her face strumming to a joyful rhythm. Her tongue rolled from side to side before swallowing reluctantly. "Been a while since I tasted something so sweet. It was singing inside my tongue."

They smiled simultaneously. Isra could feel an energy

transmitting between them. "Keep the spirits up, eh? That is what keeps you going."

"What do you mean?" Mary replied.

"Little moments like that."

"Like what?"

"What did you feel?"

"Feel?"

"Inside of you, what was the feeling?"

Mary looked over to Mousa, his back still turned away. "A warmth. I felt warmth. But not that sticky, desert warmth that clings to your clothes and sticks to your hair all the time."

"Where did you feel it?"

Mary looked around flummoxed. She stepped away from Isra.

"Point where you felt the warmth."

She pointed to her stomach and hips. "Here."

A grinding of gravel suddenly awakened Mary. It was Mousa untying one of the goats. "Over here," he pointed at her.

Her feet tapped against the ground, in short bursts that rippled through the air. Isra then watched as a blow clipped Mary on the back of the head from Mousa's stick. Mary looked down at the ground like an obedient street dog accepting its fate. She rushed over. "What was that?" she screamed.

Mousa removed the hood of the Haik. A murky outline of dimples and spots arose. "What was what?"

Isra delved deep into Mousa's retinas, and her own reflection. She could see for the first time a woman bursting through the layers of nerves. She took a step away from Mousa. "You can't keep treating her this way."

He swung the stick around, burying it into Isra's nose. "Excuse me?" he gnarled.

Isra lifted an arm and held the stick. "Beating her and treating her like muck stuck to your feet. What does that solve?"

Mousa held onto the stick, pushing it further into Isra's nostrils. "And what business is this of yours, little girl?"

Isra grabbed the stick with both hands, pushing it away from her face. "You may think we are pieces of dirt that you can play with and rule over. But let me tell you something, you horrible man. We too are human beings!"

Mousa took a step back, grinning. "Tuh! Human beings! Heard it all now. Where do you think, little girl, you would be without me, or your sorry excuse for a brother? A skeleton in the sand. That is what!"

"Do not compare yourself with my brother. He is a good person. A person with a mighty soul."

"A good person who was too weak to continue. Where is he now?"

"We will see him again."

"Isra, wake up little girl. If the soldiers did not manage to capture him, how could he survive? He can barely walk. He is in a weak position. A very weak position."

"He is right, Isra," said Mary.

"Shut up! Shut up, the both of you!"

Mousa walked over to the goats, laying out a bowl and filled it with water from a bottle. "How about being a bit more respectful of your elder."

Isra looked at Mary sitting on a large rectangular boulder. She nodded at Isra in silent resignation. Isra now for the first time felt the loss of her brother. *How is he going to hide from the soldiers? Where will he find shelter, water, food?* she pondered. For he was as tender as a new-born calf slung out of a mother's womb. Her chest felt a pricking sensation. One of longing and worry, of families abandoned to the wind and the state of her own, insignificant as it may seem, little future. She had to keep going, to light the flare for Amiin. She had to.

She gestured to Mary by scratching the back of her head. "Very well," she said.

"Once the clouds have passed, we will set up camp. There looks to be a break coming our way," said Mousa.

"But where are we going?"

"Towards the coast."

"I thought you didn't like the coastal people?"

"Who said we will be staying there?"

"Then what will we do there? We were by the coast; it can be a dangerous place."

"We won't be there long."

"How long?"

"Until we find a boat."

"A boat? To go where?"

"Little girl, you do not have to come with us. You can stay in the desert all you like."

Mary solemnly gazed at the ground. Her eyes dipped so far down all she could see were her eyelids. She scratched her head again, nodding at Mary. Despondency was spread across her face like a rash, taking her innocent young soul to the ground. She could not leave Mary to her horrible fate with Mousa, she just could not.

"Looks like this is my only choice" Isra replied, benignly.

He glided past Isra. "Keep you warm in your bed tonight" he whispered into her ear.

Isra flinched. She felt the fabric of her trousers where the flare was sleeping in her pocket. She tapped it gently, knowing that this thing that lay straight as an arrow in the inside of her cotton trousers was her only hope of seeing the ruffled curls, the warmth of his chest and the sunken, benevolent eyes that would speak to her in that calming, reassuring way that only a surrogate parent could.

It was late by the time camp was set for the night, under a row of Doum Palm trees. The sky was beginning to lift clouds away, with the bright sparks of Orion barely visible beyond the haze. Amiin had taught her about certain stars that would appear on a clear night, Orion's belt being one of them. He had three moles on his leg that looked to be in symmetry with the three stars. There were many of these stars he would recount; hiding in galaxies that were so far away it was unimaginable. He also recounted the array of colours he once saw through Mauricio's telescope; colours he did not know the words for, simmering through the lens. Again, she looked up, seeing only black, shades of grey and the pinpricks of silver.

A jackal howled into the night as Isra struggled with sleep, afraid of over-sleeping and constantly looking over her shoulder at Mousa. She looked over at the two of them, lying on their fronts like grazing sheep. She closed her eyes and drifted off to sleep.

Amiin's face appeared vividly. The contours of his face were razor sharp and the gaps between his teeth pitch black; she could almost touch the rugged stubble of his chin, curls of his declining hairline and the pearls lighting up the burnt sienna of his eyes. His countenance was foreboding, looking concerned. The contours sketched detailed features of his face: birthmarks, skin tags, freckles. He then dissipated into the night, like sand blowing in the wind. Sands of time reincarnated, tangible.

She awoke suddenly and looked at the watch, feeling very hungry. It was nine minutes until four o'clock. She unwrapped a cloth, withdrew a piece of liquorice root and chewed on it. The harsh, sweet texture of aniseed punctured into her taste buds, alleviating the hunger pains in her stomach for a few moments. She then crawled out of her sleeping bag on her stomach and tied her shoes to her feet; all the while watching the side of Mousa's head buried in the Haik.

The clouds had become denser, which blotted out the insignificant pricks of star light. She shuffled her feet away from the trees, looking for a secluded spot amongst the treacle floor that was lifting off the ground into the vast array of plumes in the sky.

The darkness thickened around her, limiting her version to a few yards. Certain sounds became magnified: Distant hyena howls, the wind blowing against rocks, the rattling of her heart inside her chest. She wandered timidly into the darkness, taking small steps, and holding her hands outright. Her leather sandals, barely clinging to her feet, scraped against stones of the path leading into a mini crater where a row of young acacia trees lined up uniformly. She looked around to where pitch black merged with the clouds. The hands of the wristwatch barely visible as the big hand hovered over the hour mark.

Her hands shook as the flare came out of her trouser pocket. She held the tube up to her eyes, to try and read the labelling on the side. A blur of the darkest green pressed into her retinas. The flare felt cold, almost frosty. Now she felt scared, a different kind of fear to before; like a lost embrace, a parting of ways, a symphony howling out to the buried stars. She remembered what Amiin had told her; scrape the wick against the ground until it lights. Hold upright between two rocks with wick facing upwards, move away. She moved sideways until the wick was burning, waiting. Suddenly it zoomed out of the ground, pinging upwards at an awkward angle towards the blanket of silver haze.

She stood bedazzled by the pastel red dot climbing. It suddenly burst in mid-air, sizzling into a flower of red petals that for a moment rooted her feet to the ground. She gawped in amazement at the beauty.

The trail of the red flower spread far into the haze, with wide reaching tentacles. The desert lit incandescently, revealing scorpions hurrying along the ground and drooping buds of cacti. The red trail then changed to plum purple before dissipating into the clouds. Gone, within seconds, as the darkness and stillness of the desert returned.

She glanced over to Mousa's sleeping area. *Did he notice?* She did not care. The only thing she cared about was if her brother had noticed the beacon of life hanging in the air; telling him that she was alive. She lumbered back to the camp with the weight of despondency and faint hope resting on her weakened shoulders. "I love you, brother," she whispered into the wind.

For a moment she thought about running away from Mousa, into the jaws of the desert. It would be easier on her own. She then remembered the scrap of dog meat, the dried vegetables, warm water, and bush plants which Mousa had acquired. It was not much but was enough to keep them going. She needed him for now, just enough to get by.

And so, they wandered the next day, with the tinkling of the goat-bell's ever fainter. Isra gazed up at the moon on clearer nights, wondering if the landscape of the other world was any different to this vast, desolate wilderness. At times she wished she were there, looking down on earth, casting an eye on the unfortunate one's toiling.

They stumbled for days from village to dwelling, into the rugged hinterland, trading goat milk for bread, corn, and drips of water. The sun was now their sole mate in the sky, peeping through the clouds on regular occasions with aplomb. The heat changed the further they travelled out of the desert; the sticky heat now replaced by fresh, gloopy drips that soaked their backs so that their clothes stuck to them like plaster to a wall. A cool breeze would brush by sporadically, lulling them into a false sense that the coast was close by.

Along the way they encountered the odd sole; with stories of brutality, pillaging and rape from the Militia. The picture painted by the Militia differed from each dwelling; from the colours of their uniform to the style of their hair, even the way they marched. The stories blew across the hinterland, becoming ever more malevolent as the salt of sea air drew ever closer. At times it seemed like they did not even exist, a mere fragment in the minds of the hungry, delirious folk.

Isra's pace became slower as the moist, basking heat intensified; sharp pains would rattle her bones and dizziness followed her into each village. She was growing weaker by the day, taking baby steps along the many roads and paths that all merged into one giant mass of sand, gravel, and cracked tarmac. Some days she would spend on her knees retching her stomach from the inside out, hoping the possessed spirit in her guts would be coughed up. This was the worst she had felt in a long time. Completely devoid of energy, enthusiasm, hope.

She chewed solemnly on a licorice bark on the morning of a particularly hot day. Her stomach had become so withered that the mere act of swallowing the juices had become a hard task.

"Where are we now?" she asked Mousa.

Mousa was sharpening a knife with a rock. "Not far from Jijiga," he replied laconically.

The goats were grazing on a piece of grass. "Jijiga? Are we in Ethiopian land?" Isra replied.

"Tuh! Ethiopian land. Many moons ago it was called that."

Isra looked around. The landscape was turning, becoming more undulating. Rocky hills sprung out of the ground, poking at jaunty angles like buildings toppled from an earthquake. Evergreen plants were appearing, weaving between rocks and growing in rows along the ground. The reddened sandy sheet was disappearing. Draknova trees mushroomed out of the ground, forming tight bundles of brown, dry leaves that curved into tulip shapes. The trees were a mysterious shape to Isra. She imagined ghosts living in the tightly formed branches. At night they would emerge as the branches opened up and fly around the desert until they had found their kindred spirits. That was what the hyenas were really howling at.

"Tell me something, child." Mousa turned around, his teeth orange from the chaat leaves. "Why did you fire that flare the other night? Do you think your brother will come and save you?"

Isra looked over to Mary. Their eyes fixed on each other for a brief second, focusing on an inner resolve, hoping. "I don't know what you mean," Isra replied.

"Ha! Please, child. Do not take me for a fool. What else lit the sky red last night?"

Isra spat the bark onto her hand. "It… it was the missiles. Did you not hear? It scared me… scared me to the bone." She could not look at Mousa. Each word an exertion on her throat, making her voice sound chaffed.

Mousa felt the blade with the tip of his finger. A drop of blood fell to the ground. "Why would the missiles be coming from the south?"

"I don't know."

"I've seen missiles and I have seen flares." He spat the leaf out. "And that was a flare."

She could feel the wrath of inquisition bearing down on her shoulders. "So, what if it was?"

"He made his choice when he left you, remember that."

"He did not leave me! He was sick."

"Sick? Is that what you call it? I have had days when I could barely breathe, and the sun would be choking the life out of me. Days when a mile made was a miracle on a drop of water. My insides would boil and out of my throat would the spawn of putrid, nasty devilment regurgitate until I was flat out on the ground and the wind in my sails gone. Poof! A lifeless carcass awaiting the vultures, which is sickness my child. But I had to keep going — for her," he pointed at Mary.

"But… he could barely walk," pleaded Isra.

"Keep telling yourself that, child. He could have walked if he really wanted to."

Mary glanced over to Isra who was making shapes in the dirt with a twig. Her disconsolance was the worst she had seen, drooping in the dirt. She stopped drawing in the dirt, facing the ground like a woman condemned to her fate. A tear fell off her chin.

"Leave her," said Mary.

"Excuse me?" Mousa replied.

"Leave her. She misses her brother is all."

Mousa marched abruptly over to Mary, with the blade pointing outwards. Mary held her stare against Mousa's glare. She fidgeted on the spot.

"You don't tell me what I can and can't say, bitch!"

"She does not need to hear it. It is a lie."

"A lie? How dare you!" The Haik extended over Mary's little body.

"Leave her, it is not a lie. I believe you, Mousa. Leave her!" Isra pleaded.

The Haik withdrew from Mary's body. She held the side of her arm, dripping blood onto the ground. Mousa shifted away from the scene, a look of disbelief permeating his face. "Shouldn't have said it! WHY DID YOU SAY THAT?"

Isra ran over to Mary. "Here, let me see," she said. The wound was in the middle of her forearm, oozing a purple sludge.

"Do you feel faint?"

Mary shook her head. Blood was now gushing out of the wound.

Isra unbuttoned her shirt, revealing flesh. She took her shirt off, wrapping it on top of the wound. "I need to press down on it. This might hurt." Mary's expression barely quivered; pain, torture, more pain, nothing new. Isra wrapped the cotton shirt around the wound then tied it together tight with the sleeves.

Mary winced. "How does that feel?" Isra asked.

"Like I am floating. Am I floating?"

"Yes, you are floating."

"Where to?"

"To the coast onto a ship and…"

"Has it stopped bleeding?" Mousa interrupted. His eyes focused on Isra's tender nipples, poking out of the side of her arms. He removed his hood and brushed his hair off his face.

"The knot should stem it for a while. We must keep the arm elevated."

Mousa looked blankly at Isra. He clamped his lips together and took a sip of water from a canister.

"Taasi waa nolosha. Waxaan u gudbaan!! Waxaan u gudbaan!!"

Isra's flesh reflected a bronze sheen in the sunlight. She crouched next to Mary, shielding her bare back from the lustful gaze of Mousa. "Can you hold this?" Isra asked. "I need to cover up."

Mousa's gaze burned into Isra like a poison arrow. "Very well."

She handed the blood-soaked sleeves to Mousa. "Keep it elevated," she said.

"It smells like rusting metal," he said.

Isra ran to her rucksack and took out another shirt. She looked down at her naked chest, wrapping around her protruding bones without an ounce of fat around the edges. She wondered what it would feel like to have that extra layer of fat, sitting around the edges of your gut. She then looked at her disappearing breasts, sinking further and further into the cavity of her chest.

Her mind focused on stabilising Mary. She threw the spare shirt around her shoulders and buttoned it up. Mousa was glaring at her. A feeling welled up inside Isra suddenly, it quivered inside of her, turning her stomach into knots. She could not look at the vile, contemptible man, she just could not. Mousa's eyes were like two beads, fixated on her and her movements. She returned to Mary and grabbed the knotted shirt off Mousa. "I think we should stay for a while. The arm needs resting."

She looked at Mary's wound. Her eyes appeared calm against the backdrop of the sun, almost cold. The colour of her arm was returning to a misty bronze, away from the cold white.

Mousa stood up, tying the goat leads to a fence post. "Very well. Your brother will not catch us either way," he said facetiously. He turned the hood back over his face and moved away.

"Where are you going?" said Isra.

"What do you care?"

"You have just stabbed Mary and now you are walking away?" Isra cowered at Mousa, awaiting the wrath.

"Do not question me, child."

"Then where are you going?"

"Are you hungry?"

"This is not about me."

"But are you hungry?"

"Yes, I am."

"I rest my case."

"Rest what case? Do you not remember sticking a knife into her flesh? What is wrong with you?"

He turned around, dwarfing her. "I will be out on the grasslands looking for rodents and snakes to cook. We need to eat, don't we? I do not see you looking. Miserable bitch."

She peered deep into his corrosive eyes, deeper than she had ventured before. A black hole appeared deep within the iris of his left eye, darker than the desert night, miles from civilization. Inside she could feel the gloopy texture of the black space, like she was wading through a pool of treacle. The blackness grew, enveloping her. A white worm creature appeared. It wriggled around the black space, hustling from side to side for an escape. It quickly grew and frenetically swiveled around the black boundary looking for an escape hole. Then, suddenly, the worm stopped moving and the blackness retreated into Mousa's eye.

"Do you want to be cut as well? Behave yourself child and listen." A spot of spit hit Isra on the cheek. "I will now hunt."

She ran away, shocked at her vision. *Amiin, where are you?* she thought. *Why did you have to become ill?* She looked towards Mousa. He smiled wryly, like he had won another battle. He had no remorse for his actions. To him, it was just existence and the daily battles he enjoyed. His way of keeping on top of the world, for his destiny was a struggle like everyone else. And the little wins he could gain; whether it was winning a petty argument, gaining a bit more milk from his goats or leaning over a vulnerable child to exert authority he would take. And Mary was just a passenger on this ride, a sterile, subservient soul who would not argue, or kick up a fuss about anything. More like a pet than a human being.

He flung a makeshift bow over his shoulder. "Give the goats some of your water. I will be a few hours," he said to Mary. He then turned to Isra with a lustful gazing. Saliva dropped from his chin onto the ground. "Look after her and I will look after you tonight, child."

Isra tightened the makeshift tourniquet on Mary's arm. A wind was blowing from the east, kicking up sand into Isra's eyes. She looked up at the clouds, where a hue of red outlined the puffy shapes, ring-fencing the clouds into neat groups. She brushed the sand away. "How does it feel?"

"Like I imagined being stabbed would feel."

"And how did you imagine it would feel?"

"Well, my arm has gone numb, but that's not bad."

"It will feel like that for a while."

"For how long?"

"A day or so, then the body will start repairing itself."

"It is amazing isn't it. The body. How it can stop hurting and heal over."

"That is what it's made to do. Kill off the old stuff and reproduce new stuff."

Mary grinned. Her eyes shined bright. "It's amazing."

Isra smiled back.

"I feel cold, though," Mary said.

Isra looked underneath the tourniquet. The skin around the wound had turned violet and looked sore. She could see the veins pulsing in the upper arm, pushing the blood out of the wound, and soaking the shirt. She tied the knot harder. "Does this hurt?"

"A little," Mary replied. "But it's fine, I'll need my arm, won't I?"

Isra smiled again. The muscles tightened around her cheeks. They felt numb, happily numb.

Chapter Nine

The soldier stumbled past Amiin, gasping in the thin air. "Nooit, nooit!" he mumbled, staggering like a drunken fool towards a row of palm trees.

"Never? What does he mean?" Amiin asked the soldier behind him.

"Ignore the fool, he is delirious," said the soldier whose copper hair poked out from under a black cap. A pubescent quality dwarfed his face; tight skin around the eyes, pointed lips, a sheen ruminating his figure. A rifle swung in the heat, pointing aimlessly towards Amiin.

Amiin's legs had grown stronger from two days of solid meals and a good supply of goat's milk. "Can I stop to pee?" he asked.

The soldier gestured to the row of palm-trees. "Be quick."

Amiin paced steadily towards the palm trees. He was feeling good. A spring was now developing in his step; every step he felt fitter, stronger.

The resurgence had happened instantaneously, waking up one day from a crippling disease only to be cured. And he felt grateful that his body was waking up once again from what felt like a long sleep. As he unzipped his trousers and felt for his penis, a shiver of optimism shot up his spine. *This is the moment!* he thought. *The moment of awakening that Mauricio proclaimed… "In adversity, the bones and the tissue and mind of your body will feel like they are shrinking into a hole in your heart. But then one day, your body says no. Enough! I want to live! And the healing process begins. Death is chased out of your veins and the soul speaks louder, clearer, faster. Arise! Carpe Diem!"*

He shook the remaining drops of urine from his penis and

zipped his flies. "Hurry up!" said the soldier. Amiin waved to the soldier. The soldier waved his rifle.

He then thought of Isra; alone with Mousa. The red flare punctuated his dreams at night. How he wished he had run as fast as he could that night to find their camp. "We will survive, Ilhama. We will be okay," he whispered slowly. He chanted it several times hoping she was listening. But he was still weak then, unable to run more than a few steps.

The groaning of his stomach and the wispy breathing of his chest rattled his bones. His eyesight was bleary from the blistering sun. *Yes,* He thought. *It was the right decision to stay with his captives until they reached the shore. Yes, it was Ilhama.* He had convinced himself that evening when every muscle in his body was willing him on. But now, amongst the cooler air he was gaining clarity. *Has she been captured? And have the goats eaten Mousa to death yet?* he pondered, wistfully.

He rejoined the Militia, counting an extra two men from the nine he had been marching with. The two appeared from nowhere as he shook his head, to shake out the hallucinations. Each soldier had a black cap glued to their heads. Underneath the shadow of their caps laid a distinct expression of subservience of will, amongst a scared little boy creeping out from under the trickle of sweat on their foreheads. He tried to guess their ages; thirteen, sixteen, twenty.

He looked at the one called Aleja, stretching his calves against a palm tree. Aleja was the tallest, with long bandy legs and a head shaped like a melon which looked too big for his body. He was the most vociferous of the group, appearing to be the leader. Aleja signalled to Amiin's minder with the copper hair and produced a wooden pipe from his trouser pocket. The group set off down a gravely track, straight towards the blaring sun. Amiin followed the man in front, with his minder perched on his shoulder. The smell of pipe smoke lingered in the air, a spicy tinge.

They had been walking for weeks, endlessly wandering in the rough, craggy hinterland as the air became cooler and the hawks screeched louder. The colours of the land were moving as evergreen plants subtly replaced the woven mix of withering bushes and dusty rocks. The sky was opening up, with mulberry spots punching through the leaden wall above. At dusk, Amiin would silently watch the colours blending into a rich tapestry trickling over the horizon.

"You are slowing down," said the minder from behind Amiin.

"Am I?" Amiin replied.

"Come, we have to keep up with the others."

Amiin turned around. "Keep going, keep going!" the minder nudged his rifle onwards then lit a cigarette.

"What is your name?" Amiin asked.

The soldier swatted a fly away from his face. "What do you care what my name is?"

"I am Amiin. From the coast."

The soldier's face turned crimson. He looked around, focusing on a hawk perched on a telegraph pole. "What is a name? I could be a number. Three, four, one for all you care."

"Then where do you come from?"

The soldier looked towards the top of the group where Aleja had his back turned. "Old Mogadishu."

"All the way from Mogadishu?"

"Keep your voice down, damn you!" the soldier barked.

"I thought Mogadishu was in a fairly good state compared to other parts of the land. Why did you leave?"

"If that's so, why didn't you move to there?" the soldier replied.

"We… well, my sister and I thought about it. I was not keen on the old cities. Heard terrible stories."

"And the coastal dwellings are much better?"

"You tell me."

"I have never been to the coast."

"And is that where we are going?"

The soldier shrugged his shoulders. "I believe so."

The soldier waved the rifle butt towards the other soldiers. "It's Jos by the way."

The scraping of shoes on gravel awoke a vulture from an Acacia tree that was leaning over a cliff face. Amiin noticed the leaves of the Acacia's more evergreen than the desert trees. The trunks were also fatter, almost muscular, with branches overarching to the ground. It was not just the Acacia trees that were different; the soil was darker, rich like coffee grounds and the grasses thicker with the entanglement of other plants he had not seen for a long time. Poinsettia Flowers popped up between the hardy grasses — dots of pink that instantly grabbed his attention. The Cacti were shaped differently to the desert; wider, squarer, with a thicker mass around the base.

That night they camped in a disused warehouse made of rusting tin. They approached the warehouse at dusk, with an amber glint gently warming the western half of the sky. Amiin had lost track of their whereabouts — for the tracks they were now treading along he did not recognise. The tracks seemed to weave around the hinterland smoothly, like a sand-snake coiling along the slippery sand. And each turn took him further into a tunnel, further from Isra.

He could not sleep. The corroded metal walls rattled with the wind and the sound of crickets from outside. It was getting warmer at night, away from the dry coldness of the desert night. He pulled the sleeping bag back, stretching his legs. A soldier immediately walked over to him. He had scars crisscrossing around his face and tendrils of hair poking out of a sweaty cap.

He waved a rifle butt loosely "back to bed". In the darkness Amiin could clearly see a white, blue, and red flag on the tip of his cap.

"I can't sleep," Amiin replied.

The soldier took his cap off and wiped his brow. He shrugged and lit a cigarette.

"Can I get some fresh air? Feel a bit sick," Amiin said.

The soldier took a long drag of the cigarette and blew a thick cloud of smoke into the holed wall. "Five minutes then back to bed. Otherwise, Aleja will string me up."

He tied his moccasin shoes together and moved towards a gap in the tin-panel walls with the soldier lumbering behind.

He took a deep breath, the air cooling his lungs. In the distance he could see a sprinkling of light; electric, candles, fire? It was hard to tell. He made out among the faded light the tops of high hills stretching for miles like the back of a scaly lizard; jagged and serrated. The verdant of the grasslands added an extra sheen to the landscape, like the glow of a lake in the darkest of nights.

The smell of the grass was crisp, moist, lining the tip of his tongue with a dewy freshness. He looked up at the clouds, and could see the moonlight strengthening nightly, casting a white veneer as the celestial lump of rock waited patiently for the clouds to pass. He waited with anticipation for a full moon to appear.

His memory of the moon was becoming hazy, remembering the phases. The blood moon, appearing on rare occasions, was the phase he remembered the most. Each day the moon was different, as if the sun were snacking on the rim, before letting the rim grow back over the nights. Various stages, colours, positions. It was enchanting to him as a boy.

"Do you long to see him again?" said Amiin.

"Who?" then let out a ring of smoke.

"The man in the sky," he pointed.

"How do you know it's a man?"

Amiin kicked stones on the ground. "I just know. He is like my friend of the night."

"And why not a woman?"

"Has a face like a man; thick chin, stern eyes, the outline of a beard."

The soldier smirked. "You talk nonsense."

Amiin stared at the child soldier. His skin appeared milky in the darkness. "How old are you?"

The soldier waved the rifle at Amiin. His eyes furtively looked to the ground for a distraction. "Why? You need to stop asking questions and hurry up with your business."

"Do you even know?"

"Know what?"

"Your age?"

The soldier lit another cigarette and looked upwards. "How big does it get?"

"The moon?"

"Yes, I hear so much about it. What is it? Where did it come from?"

Amiin wiped down a wooden crate that had been left outside. A sheet of dust blew into the wind. He sat on it. "I only know what I heard from an old friend I knew for a brief time. It is a massive ball of rock, like our planet but much smaller. It controls the tides of our seas and the wind in the sky. It appears every night in different forms, depending on when the sun shines against the side. So, some days it will be full of yellow and others a different shape, like a smile in the sky. It is a world not like ours, we could not live there."

"Why can't we live there?"

"Something to do with the air. It would kill us all."

"And how would you get there? By aeroplane?"

"A rocket."

"What's a rocket?"

"Something that goes really, really fast. It has to get out of the earth. Through a thing called the atmosphere."

"Like a flare?"

"Something like that yes."

"And the atmos—?"

"—phere, atmosphere. It is what you see in the sky, well kind of. It protects the planet from meteorites and evil spirits."

"I heard about meteorites. They are also rocks that come from space, aren't they?"

"That's right. God hurls them at us when he's unhappy."

The soldier sat down next to Amiin; his eyes glazed. "Why would he be unhappy with us?"

Amiin opened his mouth but could not answer the question. "Lots of reasons, lots and lots."

The soldier turned his back on Amiin and checked inside the warehouse for movement. The rifle was left on the wooden crate, right next to him. He thought about shooting the boy. It would be over in a second and he could flee back to Isra.

But he was miles away from this point, hundreds of miles. He had lost count of the amount of abandoned buildings and cactus plants they had passed. And Isra's face was now beginning to fade from his memory. The eyes were clear, but the outline of her face was fading into the night. He put a hand on the rifle butt. It was icy cold. The coldness penetrated his nerves, for he had no idea how to handle or shoot a rifle.

He realised his best hope of finding Isra was to wait and hope that she would find him, by some kind of miracle.

"How long before we reach our destination?" Amiin whispered.

"A few days Aleja says."

"Can I?" Amiin pointed at the soldier's cigarette.

The cigarette end glowed orange as the soldier passed it to Amiin. He took a puff, coughing. The tension in his heart eased as a side of the moon (a cheek punctuated with craters) punched through the clouds.

Chapter Ten

As the first yelps of the hyenas the following morning Amiin awoke to a sudden din of activity from outside; boots shuffling against gravel, bags scraping against tarmac, voices yelping at one another until the noise of a crowd manifested. "Hurry, pack up the mess tins!" "The rations! Don't forget the biscuits!"

Aleja appeared at Amiin's bedside with a strong kick to the foot. His face had a purple tinge to it, specifically around the eyes where the lids hung heavy. He played with the buttons of his shirt, twirling the thread around his fingers. "Up, wake up!" he shouted.

Amiin immediately sat up. "What is happening?"

"We are moving."

"Where are we going?"

Aleja turned his head to the side. His eyes became narrow, focusing on a trampled piece of cardboard on the floor. A fist arose, striking Amiin on the cheek. Amiin's head reeled back in shock.

"You don't get to ask questions… Aleja's eyes burned bright… remember that." He signalled with his hand to move off the cardboard bed.

Tin cans littered the floor, spilling gloopy liquid onto the cold concrete floor. Amiin packed up his belongings into a Bergen rucksack and looked around the warehouse. The soldiers busied themselves, hastily packing away provisions off the floor like hungry, scavenging mice. "Help them… damn you!" a soldier shouted into Amiin's face.

"What is happening?"

"The mighty one is chasing us, that is what. We must escape the damnation!" the soldier pointed to the sky, kissing his fingers. "Help me pack the sheets."

Amiin followed the soldier known as Didshassi around the floor with the Bergen. Didshassi had acquainted himself with him two days ago during a campfire by stroking his knee and whispering lewd words into his ear. He looked different to the others, with paler skin and longer, wavy hair dripping over his shoulders.

Didshassi crammed sheets into the Bergen, then tied a cord around the bag and threw it to the floor. Amiin noticed glints of silver as he tied the Bergen. Glints that shone brightly for a brief second inside the rucksack. Didshassi pushed Amiin and told him to get outside. As he stumbled outside, he turned, to see Didshassi peering inside the rucksack.

A stream of hot air rushed across his cheek as he rushed past cracked walls, dusty shelves, and rusting machine parts into the parched air. He coughed, his breath shallow. A brightened tint flashed before his eyes, increasing with each step forward until his eyes closed. The blue hue rushed into the blackness of space beyond his own consciousness like the tide lapping up an exposed piece of beach. He opened his eyes gingerly. The grey clouds were cast aside, with an aquamarine cover now asphyxiating the sky into a rapid hold. Amiin looked upon the new horizon in awe. He grinned broadly and thought of Isra, the beautiful blue.

The soldiers lined up in a ragtag formation outside the warehouse. A tired, long-lost look graced the soldiers' faces, as if they were about to go into an unwinnable battle. Amiin turned his attention to a ravaged dog circling around the soldier's feet for scraps of food. The dog's yelp then pierced the parched air, as a plethora of boots kicked the dog's hind.

"Enough!" Aleja shouted from inside. His voice sounded reedy. The soldiers stood still, their boots moving away from the dog. Aleja then appeared, with a sweaty green bandana across his forehead. Didshassi followed behind Aleja, his shadow appearing at the side like a hemorrhoid.

Aleja moved to the front of the soldier's line. "Right, now is the time my brothers. Now is the time!" a graveled octave manifested in his voice.

"For so long the mighty one has chased us. Chased us through the deserts while the vultures circle, chased us through our homes while our brothers and sisters sleep, chased us to the brink… where each one of us looked death in the face!" He paused, coughing. Didshassi patrolled the front rank, looking deep into the bloodshot lines of the soldier's weary eyes.

"Well, no more, my brothers. We retreat for the last time! It is folly to suggest otherwise! Today the almighty one has made the declaration, we take the fight to the hills for the last time! The red demon will chase us no more! Anyu la dagaallanno! Waxaan ku tagaan! Anyu la dagaallanno! Waxaan ku tagaan!" The soldiers awoke from their slumber, tapping their boots into the ground until a dust-cloud gathered around their feet.

"We move to the hills now. Where we will rain hellfire onto the red demon's army!" Aleja picked a rifle off the floor, wiped down the barrel with a cloth and fired into the air. "Our Lord chose us to bring the fight on this day. This day he chose when the clouds would part and show us. Our lord speaks clearly to us today, no ambiguities, no false dawns. Blood will be spilled for him TODAY!"

The din of boots tapping the ground grew louder as Aleja and Didshassi each produced a pocket knife. They both waved a finger in the air, cutting the fingertip. They then held their bloodied fingers aloft and shoved the finger in each other's mouth, Didshassi sucking Aleja's finger like a baby suckling its thumb for the first time.

"Do the same for your brothers!" Aleja released his finger from Didshassi's mouth. Didshassi handed out four pocket knives to the front row. The soldiers in the front row grabbed at the knives, Aleja then produced a rolled-up piece of paper from his shirt pocket. The paper was wrapped in a ribbon like an ancient scripture. His gaze was jittery, focusing on the hills beyond the back entrance of the warehouse. As he untied the ribbon his fingers shook. The soldiers cut their fingers and placed them into each other's mouths. Aleja turned his focus on the group, focusing on Amiin.

He unrolled the paper. "Our Lord, who looks down upon his soldiers with pride, love, and compassion. Our Lord who is our protector. Our Lord who seeks to deliver justice to those who sin, and who will deliver the apocalypse on the sinners who try to dehumanise our world. For our world is a simple world, where all we ask for is love amongst our brothers and sisters. Our Lord will protect us when on this day, this most auspicious of days the day of reckoning will come. This day the sun god will give us the signal, to attack with all our rage and venom at the sinners who try to extinguish our brothers and our way of life from our earth. Who are the invaders? Who are the sinners crossing the desert? They are faceless men, with mighty weapons no doubt. But my brothers, we have us, we have a bond. A bond that will never be broken for as long as the bullets rain down on our shoulders we stand together. An army of one..." he took a breath, sipping on a water canister. Didshassi looked at Aleja, drooling.

"If one falls, we do not stop to take the fallen one's hand. We let them be, for the Lord will look after the fallen brother in a rosy Babylon. We carry on fighting; with bullets, bombs, fists, and fingernails until the sinners have been pushed back to their ungodly hole."

"Let's go" Didshassi barked at the soldiers.

Amiin picked the Bergen off the ground, flinging it over his shoulders. Despite the jingoistic bombast a new horizon was forming for him. This was a moment for him to take back control of his life and find Isra again. Night after night he looked to the sky, in the vein hope of finding the flare.

"Let's go," the words rang in his head. *Always running, but what from? Who was the latest enemy?* It felt like his whole life was about running, physically and spiritually, from the evils in the world. Running from hunger, famine, pain, murderers, predators, running to food, to water, to shelter. He had forgotten what it was like to call anything a home.

Suddenly a roar crackled in the sky, cascading from the

eastern shores. He listened acutely. The sound resembled a desert prince singing to his mistress amongst an ensemble of dignitaries. Well, that was how he imagined it. A scurrying, scraping sound rumbled along the ground, shaking his ribs. It sounded like monsters burrowing into his feet.

Then the explosion came. He glanced over to Aleja just before the first casualty was born in the hinterland winds. His face had turned orange and his expression seemed to move out of the lines of his face. It was an expression born into another time and place which he could not figure out. A high pitch descended, then silence.

The battle had arrived.

Chapter Eleven

Isra sat gazing intently on the horizon, body still, waiting for the blue river about to trickle into the sky.

She opened a can of beans, thrusting a rock at the lid and ripping the tin with her fingers. A thin veil of gloop trickled out of the top. A blue cloak began to slowly take over the sky, in dots and specks, swamping the white patches. The brightest blue hue that lit up the sky like nothing she had seen before. Pure sky blue. It was beautiful beyond words.

She turned to look at the sun behind her, shielding her eyes while the mighty star winked. And there it was, laid out before her, the painting of which she had dreamed. Amiin had said it was like seeing the ocean upside down, but brighter, calmer. This was a painting like no other. For beyond the blue, she could make out traces of other stars and the faded crescent of the moon. She thought the description was crazy at the time but now it made sense.

Mary lumbered out of a sleeping bag behind Isra. "Aiii so it happened!"

Isra remained quiet, deep in thought. Her mother and father were talking to her now that the clouds had passed. She closed her eyes and heard voices from her childhood, very distinct and clear: *Her mother telling her to wash behind the ears and not slurp her water. Her father's voice echoed in the distance, a faint memory of early years; gruff, hoarse, and full of vitality.* She closed her eyes and imagined him: *a tall, well-built man with a shaggy mop of hair and a thinly veiled moustache. Casting a net in his small fishing boat, bare chested, then watching the sun set into the ocean before pulling up the nets of tender fish. He smiled at Isra, exposing high gums, and cracked teeth.* The image then faded into the thick, turquoise sea above.

"A thing of beauty…" Isra opened her eyes. "…it's every bit as enchanting as Amiin said."

"Everything looks different. It's like the sun is lighting the land through a blue torch or something," said Mary. Mary's skin appeared opaque, resembling a semblance of health. Isra could smell a fragrance on her breath of apples; delicious, juicy, fresh apples. She looked into Mary's eyes and sensed hope.

The cut arm hung loosely by her side. It swung limply in the wind, like the dead branch of a tree. Mary looked down at the wound, looking like a crater in the ground, a fuchsia tint. The wound needed constant attention from her, at one point she thought the arm was lost due to infection, but miraculously it had survived. Every day Isra had managed to find new dressings amongst the dumped litter and uninhabited shacks they had passed through. When the wound had to be cleaned, she would sacrifice her own water canister and when Mousa barked at her to leave Mary alone she stood firm.

Despite her disability Mary chirped on with the daily slog of life. Her doleful expressions and innocent gazing at the world pushed Isra on. For this was one fight, for Mary, she was determined to win.

Mary sloped past Isra, a few paces back to the tent where they were camped. Their spirits were high due to the feast of goat they had devoured the night before. Mousa had given the order reluctantly to slaughter one of the goats; his beloved goats whom he held in the highest regard. But he knew that sustenance was the most pressing issue of their voyage now. In the days leading up to the sacrifice there had been multiple collapses, including himself, whose body had resembled a decaying Leadwood tree. He hung over the weakest goat, peering deep into the realms of the goat's gloopy eyes and plunged a knife through its heart. The goat was given a proper send off, a strange ritual where Mousa danced naked around the corpse before covering it in sand. He then sat motionless beside the lifeless animal, staring up at the stars that were sparkling down on the spirit departed.

"Let us not get too distracted. We have a lot to do today — remember?" said Isra. She led Mary away from the blue horizon and back into the boulder valley. They descended a few metres into a vast ravine of boulders and ground shrubs. Their camp was sheltered by a group of Acacia trees pointing to the east. The tree branches drooped inwards, creating ripples of shade along the ground.

Mousa was cleaning pots with an oily rag. "What were you looking at?"

Isra wiped her mouth with her baggy shirt sleeve. "What else would we be looking at?"

"It won't last once the dust clouds gather."

"I thought water was in the clouds. Isn't that where water comes from?" Mary asked.

Mousa turned towards Mary. "The water clouds deserted us some time ago, child."

"But will they come back now that the blue is here?"

"When the gods decide."

"Decide what?"

"To send the rain clouds toward us and banish the dust clouds to a faraway place."

Mary looked at Isra, hoping for validation. Isra looked away, to the horizon that was pocketed into a smaller space above them over the shadow of the tree.

The sky to her had always been monstrous dust clouds, hanging over her very existence her whole life. The blue sky, whilst beautiful beyond imagination felt discombobulating, dizzying. Questions formed in her head. *Would it bring the rains that had been talked about for years over the campfires and bedtime stories? What did the gods want in return?*

And did they even need these sponges of moisture to rain on them?

She smirked, breathing in new, fresher air. She then turned towards Mary. "When you see a hyena scurrying along the road what do you see?"

Mary's brow scrunched up. "What do you mean?"

"What do you see?"

"An animal sniffing for things."

"And what is it sniffing for?"

"Food I suppose, or other hyenas."

Isra looked over to Mousa. His back turned with shoulders sloped but she could tell he was listening. "And what else?"

"I don't know… shelter, comfort?"

"That is right, but there is another answer that combines all of your answers…" she held her two index figures into the air. "It's just we don't know what we are looking for, except a mean existence. They can smell the answer in the air. One which takes all our basic needs and gives it all purpose. For the hyena just like every other living thing is looking for that one simple answer."

"And what does that have to do with the rains?"

"My point is, they are not waiting for the rain clouds to come. They just get on."

"Get on with what?"

"Existing."

Mary shook her head. "Existing?"

"And while they are existing, they look for the answer. It is the only way."

The sides of Mary's face scrunched inwards into a compressed ball. She looked despondent, yet angry. "I am bored of existing. When do we get to live? I may only be a child to you and to him, but I have feelings too! All I have done is move; from shack to shack, tent to tent, and all for what?"

Isra took a step back, a surprised hatching flustering her face. "Be quiet or he will hear you."

"It's just…" Mary's jaws drooped. "I am tired, Isra. Where are we? What are we doing? I'm so tired."

"For now, we just concentrate on the here and now, not the future." She held Mary by the shoulders and stroked her hair with her long, jagged fingernails. She glanced at the months of sandy dirt piling up underneath the calcium lacquer, remembering not so long ago how much pride she took in her fingernails.

Out of the corner of her eye she could see Mousa slowly walking down a rock face to where the last remaining goat lay still. She thought about picking up the nearest boulder and knocking him over. She thought about stabbing him in the night. She even contemplated knocking him out cold and feeding him to the goats. This man, this retched human being, was the one major obstacle to hers and Mary's wellbeing. He was the one blocking all their paths. He was the one pervading their very existence into a ground up emancipation of shackled anger and lost hope.

Like the dust clouds he was never far away, always controlling. A destiny maker pounding both of their wills into his own mould. For his destiny was an ever-evolving cobweb, like an ever-expanding galaxy. And like stars fading into new orbits his cobweb was about to consume their destiny into his own orbit. For he would have his own way, and they were subservient to his wills.

The dust clouds passing presented an opportunity. This was the sign Isra had been waiting for. "I have a plan. Tonight, we will be free."

That evening they settled down to a familiar routine of cleaning clothes and lighting a fire, while the blue ocean emptied out of the sky and the temperature dipped. The night was a clear one, with stars beginning to emerge. Thousands of stars, as far as the eye could see. They both gawped at the formations of stars they had not seen before: lines, diamonds, squares, noticing tight formations that looked like mini clouds of stars.

"Galaxies," Isra said. "I think the mini clouds are galaxies."

"What are galaxies?" Mary asked.

"Millions, billions of stars I've been told."

"They look close together."

"I do not think they are. Quite the opposite."

The crescent moon coaxed into the pitch black of night as Mary gathered sticks from the lower side of the ravine.

The stocks of kindle were running low, so Isra resorted

to rubbing sticks together. The fire eventually came, purple sparks brushing the ground. Mary sat next to the fire, feeling the warmth gliding gently across her cheeks. Isra rustled in her rucksack for the day's provisions of food, a can of dates in syrup with some hard crusts of bread. Mousa sat to one side cross-legged, gently gnawing on some goat meat. He had decided the meat would only be for his consumption today, purely on a whim.

He appeared withdrawn today, barely saying a word. The hood of his Haik seemed even tighter around his head, almost suffocating him. Isra could feel an undercurrent of venom coiling up underneath the Haik. It coiled inside her stomach, making her nauseous.

"Pass me the salt," he murmured.

Isra handed Mousa a brown packet which he snatched from her grasp.

"Thanks," she said facetiously.

"And what do I thank you for?" Mousa replied.

"It's just polite to say thanks."

"Tuh! Since when?"

"That is what we did in our village."

"And for what is there to be thankful? Handing over a bag of salt? Your cheek knows no boundaries sometimes, child."

"They call it manners."

Mousa adjusted the hood. "Are you trying to bamboozle me with some stupid customs? This is not your village now, you little whore!"

Mary tapped her on the shoulder, their eyes met. "It doesn't matter," Isra said, crestfallen.

A look of subtle triumph ringed Mousa's eyes. "I should string you up for such intolerance and feed you to the hyenas." As he spoke his tongue glowed red, flittering between words like a flame in the wind. "Who IS your master, Isra of the beach? Tell me!"

Isra looked at Mary, who nodded to the ground. "You are my master." She looked to the ground for salvation. The hyenas howled in the background, mocking her submission.

Mousa stood up. "Go to that tree," he said, pointing to a Baobab tree jutting out of the hillside.

"Why?"

Mousa's Haik shadowed over the fire. "Are you questioning your master?"

Isra again looked at Mary, nodding with intent. She then tenderly threw a woollen scarf around her neck, got to her feet, and tied her hair into a tight bun. She walked in a straight line towards the tree like a soldier on parade; *just another task to be done.* But she knew what was coming. A tongue rasping against her cheeks, brittle stubble rubbing against her skin. She would obey, though, for the sake of the plan, the almighty plan. *Amin, this is all for you.*

She stopped at the base of the tree trunk and sat down with her back turned, just as the light from the fire had dimmed. She removed her scarf with shoulders shivering against the wind.

Mary looked on. She had seen her master, Mousa, treat people mean. But something felt different this time. This time she could feel real venom in his voice and raging animosity from his eyes. "Keep an eye on him," he pointed to the sleeping goat.

He paced over to the tree, legs clambering over the rocks like a bandy ostrich. "Take off your clothes, NOW!" he shouted. Mary stood by, helplessly watching Mousa manhandle Isra's scarf and cotton top off her body. Isra kept her back turned, slowly peeling off her dress. Mary looked at the goat. The goat's eyes were firmly shut, like it was conveniently ignoring the horrors about to unravel. She felt like she was in an ocean, the current pulling her body further from Isra's.

"No!" she screamed. "Nooooo!!!"

Mousa kissed Isra's bare neck, slobbering over the flesh. Isra complied, sitting in the same position like she was praying at a voyeur moon. He pushed her head forward, exposing her skinny bottom and withering thighs. "I will teach you once and for all who your master is – Isra of the beach," he whispered into her ear.

Like a marble statue lying still in the dead night, she obeyed.

His body locked into hers, pinning the prey to the ground. Her gaze veered off up the hill where the faint moon smiled. A scorpion crawled along the ground a few yards away, nonchalantly. For a moment Isra thought about the scorpion and how they mated, how much it could hurt and whether there was any joy in it at all. Mousa threw the Haik to the ground and lay on top of Isra. His body, all skin and bones looked fuller in the moonlight as his arms pressed Isra's shoulders to the ground. "I am your MASTER. I am your MASTER!" he chanted.

The words floated across the ravine, spectral. She looked for the scorpion before closing her eyes but could see nothing but a black screen with pinpricks of starlight peeping through. *Will be over soon, soon.* Her father's face briefly appeared, then her mother's.

His body then suddenly toppled onto one side as she felt a weight lifted off her back.

She looked over at Mousa clutching his shoulder blade. She then looked up and saw Mary with a frightful look glazing her eyes, like she had witnessed the end of the world. A red knife fell out of her hand to the ground. Mousa grappled on the ground, thrashing his head from side to side "AAAAAARRRGGGHH!" he cried. A pool of blood formed around his feet.

"What, whaaaat have you done?" Isra said, panicked.

Mary picked the blade off the ground and ran to the tent while Mousa kneeled on the ground, scrambling his fingers along his shoulder blade. In the moonlight his bare shoulders pierced the darkness, exposing his mighty body back to a crumpled state.

"Arrrrrggghh. You bitch!" he howled, fumbling around the wound. A panicked look blazed his face, as if the many scrapes with death were finally catching him.

Isra immediately ran after Mary, oblivious to Mousa's yelps of anguish.

Mary sat next to the goat, calmly wiping the knife with a rag. "What was that?" she shouted.

Mary spat on the blade, wiping the metal until it was clean. She held it up against the phosphorescent moonlight, turning it from side to side. The goat got to its feet and yawned, a laconic yawn that held time on its tongue. Isra looked first at the goat and then at Mary, her expression indifferent.

"Shall we go?" Mary asked.

"Go?"

"Yes, go."

"Go where?"

"You decide, being the elder."

Isra looked across the ravine at Mousa's body kneeling towards the moon. His hands were now by his side, static. "What about him?"

Mary stood up. Her face glowed silver, lips turned inwards. She handed the knife to Isra. "You decide."

Isra took a step back. Droplets of sweat dropped off her forehead into the cracks of the rocks. She looked down at the rocks by her feet, ragged, sharp, millions of years old. She wondered how many forms of life had trod on these exact rocks and where the rock originally came from. Tales of mountains spitting blistering hot rocks out of the ground had passed the generations. She remembered her mother telling her of one such mountain, called a volcano in the Ethiopian lands that erupted one day, wiping out many villages with rivers of piping hot liquid called lava. She visualised the rage burning inside the mountain, like a coiled spring about to burst.

She then took a rock in her quivering hands, stroking the serrated edges like she was running her fingers through a rabbit's silky fur. The metronome of her heartbeat pounded, heavy. Something was boiling inside the pit of her stomach, churning, bubbling. Her head spun, gliding around the stars until a pop went off beside her ear. She then gripped the rock tightly and ran over the rocks where Mousa lay.

His body lay to one side, while his rear seeped into the ground with a river of blood.

"Nolol Jaro! Nolol Jaro!" he mumbled. The Haik hung loose from his head, covering his mangled hair. She stepped into his line of sight. One side of his face was dipping into his chin and his eyes were in a state of blinking flux. Towering over his dying body Isra puffed out her chest and broadened her shoulders. She now had the power. A resounded look now plagued Mousa as he lay against a rock with blood pouring out of his shoulder; the look of destiny catching up with the immortal. His eyes focused on the distance where not so long ago he was a healthier man, with a purpose in life.

Something crawled into the corner of Isra's eye line, down by her feet. It was a scorpion, much bigger than the one she had seen before. The scorpion moved over a pile of rocks then stopped in between the cracks, like it was waiting for something. She bent down to inspect it. The scorpion backed away, tail cocked like a rifle, with the stinging ball ready to inject death. She backed away. In the black space behind the rocks, she could make out tiny dots of light; two beady eyes assiduously surveying the situation.

She turned to Mousa, removing the Haik from his head, and looked deep into his eyes in the moonlight.

His pupils were dilated, exposing orange flashes. She delved into the whites of his eyes, searching for something, anything, a sign. A gateway into the depths of Mousa's soul. The man who had spent his entire life herding goats across the desert and living for nothing but instant gratification against the most vulnerable. To deflower a virgin or to kill a man? Accepted in his brutal world. For him there was a code of charred reason behind inhuman acts. *What was in Mousa's DNA?* She peered further and further into his eyes, looking for a reason. *Why did this man take my virginity? Why? Why?* The voice in her head screamed. She began to cry, letting out a harsh shrill. The shrill leapt around the rocks, like a gunfight. The voice grew, poking her by the ears. *What was his reason? Why did he treat me like a lump of meat?*

She shook her head to try and dislodge the voice, but it would not disappear. Her temple shook violently as he continued to chant, "Nolol Jaro! Nolol Jaro!" while blood continued to stream from his body onto the ground. The patch of claret expanded darker, thicker in the moonlight, as if the patch were consuming his body whole.

The chanting then stopped abruptly. He sat up, raising his head towards the sky as she watched intently. He then moved his hips towards her and shuffled his legs. A flame appeared in each eye, burning blue. She took a step back, startled.

"Isra of the beach," he said, shaking his head. She threw her arms into the air as the rock crashed down on his forehead.

The noise of the skull cracking was oddly subdued, like a small nut cracking. His body fell sideways, sloping to the ground with arms flayed out. Isra stood over his head and rained another heavy blow to the skull. A pool of blood emerged around his shoulders, lapping up the dead air. Another blow crashed down on his skull, this time dislodging pieces of bony mucus onto the ground. "Nolol ja…" he mumbled for the last time, his hands hanging loose.

The final blow almost split Mousa's skull in two. His body immediately slumped to the ground, with face buried in a pile of stones.

Isra peered into the bloody mess. Gone were the hangdog eyes, slippery countenance. The Haik hung loose around his ears, blowing gently in the wind. Brain tissue and dark sludgy liquid. The head was no longer circular, more an extended oval with the entire roof caved in. And with the deformed wreck of a head now facing Isra she could see that the man Mousa; the nomad, goat-herder, bully, rapist had passed into the night. His existence no longer on this land. No longer could he clamp down and press her conscience into the dirt. As the relief and sorrow toiled in her mind the scorpion emerged again, ready for a meal.

She sat down next to his feet, buried her face in her elbows and cried into the bright canvas of night.

Chapter Twelve

The last flare faded in the daylight; an orange puff that evaporated into the white clouds like foam hissing on a riverbank.

Amiin watched the residue gently falling back to earth, hoping that Isra had seen it. He winced, looking around the cave. "Pass me the water," he said.

Red tints glowed in the cave from a young man in military fatigues who threw a plastic bottle at Amiin. "How is the leg?" the soldier asked. Amiin looked down at the side of his right shin where a dark patch oozed through his green trousers. The wound was a palette of violet that changed with each drop of sunlight that escaped into the dark recess.

He unzipped the fly and rolled down the right leg to where the wound throbbed; he closed his eyes he could hear his own pulse reverberating round and round the cave. He unscrewed the bottle top, dropping water on the wound.

"Still functioning," Amiin said, stoically.

"Pass me that rag will you," he flexed the wounded leg.

The boy soldier stood up, walking slowly around the charcoaled feet of a corpse. As he walked around the body half covered in dried leaves and bloody towels, he signalled with two fingers to the roof of the cave and briefly glanced upwards. He then passed a bloodied rag to Amiin. "Need a hand with that?" he asked.

Amiin reluctantly nodded, wincing.

The soldier leant down and wrapped the rag around the wound, then pulled hard and tied it into a tight knot. Amiin bit his lip, the pain pouring out of his mouth. "Damn! Damn!" he let out a long breath. "Not getting any easier this is it?" He reached for the water bottle and took a sip.

"What are we going to do with Mak?" said the boy soldier.

"So, he had a name?" Amiin wiped sweat off his brow in one long swoop. "Well, we either have to leave or bury him somewhere. The smell is starting to make me gag."

The boy moved over to Mak's head, removing some of the leaves. Two mackerel eyes peered back. The boy peered into the deadened pupils unshaken. "Did he die for a good cause?"

"A good cause?"

"Yes. Was his life taken for a good reason?"

Amiin pulled his trouser leg back up to his waist. "I suppose so."

The boy placed the leaves back over the eyes. His expression was as deadpan as the corpse that lay in front of him. "And what was that cause?"

"Why don't you ask your illustrious leader? Oh, I forgot he can't help us right now can he!" Amiin snapped.

"Aleja said we were messengers for the mighty one. And that if our lives were taken by the barbarians we would be rewarded."

"Well, there you go then."

"You sound like you don't believe what Aleja said?"

Amiin took a sip of the water and gazed out of the mouth of the cave. They were high on the hillside, looking down at orange rock faces and grassy patches below where goats fed. The rock faces deep with sharp inclines. He could see the sun, burning brightly above the hills. Another blue sky filled the horizon, but this sky was different to the one he had seen when the attack happened. It had an emerald tinge to it, like the water of the Red Sea. "I tell you what I believe. What is your name?"

"Sixteen."

"No, your name, what's your real name?"

"I told you, Sixteen."

"As in the number?"

"Yes."

"Why Sixteen?"

"It was the number Aleja gave me when he rescued me."

"Well, okay, Sixteen. Here is what I think. See that flare I fired off?"

Sixteen nodded obediently.

"That is all I care about right there. For that is the only hope I have of finding my sister — the only reason I must live. You can talk to me all day about Aleja's beliefs, but it doesn't steer me from my sister."

"But many of us died fighting for these beliefs, there must be some reason — surely?" Sixteen looked at Amiin, a disbelieving panic enveloping his eyes.

Amiin looked at the youth of Sixteen; ginger tips of curls on his cranium, clear patches of milky skin under his eyes like clean rivers, knees bent loosely and acrobatic. Sixteen's eyes glazed as he stared at death before his very eyes. Amiin felt a pity for him.

"Where are you going now?" Amiin asked.

Sixteen stared at the corpse. "I do not know."

"Well, once the leg has healed why don't you join me?"

"But where will you go to find your sister? What about food, water?"

Amiin slapped his leg. "I've come this far and I'm still standing — just about!" he laughed.

Sixteen slapped his own leg, he laughed too. The echo of laughter filled the cave rapturously. "Very well, Amiin, very well!" The laughter continued as slaps exchanged throughout the afternoon and into the clear, effervescent twilight.

Sixteen tossed uncomfortably in the cave that night. The gunfight still clear in his mind...

Barrages of shells raining down on their position as red smoke filled the night sky. "They're coming I can see them," the sentry shouted.

"Well, let them know we are waiting for them — fire! But be cautious with your bullets! The mighty one is watching your back remember!" Aleja shouted.

Minutes seemed like days as Sixteen lay in a ditch waiting for the oncoming rush — the 'enemy'. But Sixteen had no clue as to what the enemy looked like. Were they dark skinned or light? Did they have uniforms? Did they have brothers and sisters like he once had? And what god were they fighting for? Aleja had told the group about barbarity against their own families; of throats slit while their children played outside, of animals slayed for no reason and of elders herded into locked warehouses and burnt to death. This meant nothing to Sixteen, though, he was a six-year-old boy living off the burnt remains of cockroaches and wild grasses when Aleja's army found him one day. He had no recollection of anything resembling parents. All he had was a brother and two sisters, who were separated from him when a rival gang had raided their village at a young age. Sixteen could still hear the screams of his older sister the day he had run... "Go! Just go before they take you... PLEEEEASE." Then a horrid mute before the screaming began.

Sixteen then wandered around the wilderness like a stray dog. When Aleja first ran into this grubby little boy, he had been surprised by how feral he was. He had even tried to bite Aleja the first time they had met. He named him Sixteen due to the number of seconds it had taken for him to withdraw his fangs from Aleja's foot.

It was dusk when the real bullets were fired. The enemy eventually appeared, raining heavy gunfire down on their position. Sixteen aimed his rifle towards the orange flashes and billows of smoke, waiting for faces to appear, towards a gigantic rock face where the enemy hid behind. Then the bombs rained down, one hundred yards from Sixteen's position. The bombs fizzed in the air, clouded in giant smoke screens before burying into the sandy soil like giant earthworms digging.

Violet spit flew out of Didshassi's mouth. "Ready, Sixteen? We've got the bastards this time!" he shouted, spitting chaat residue onto the ground. Sixteen glanced over to Didshassi's face, noticing a covering of sweat on his forehead. "Our Lord will rain hellfire on all of you dogs! Come on, you bastards, come to the gates of hell. We welcome you! Come!" he screamed, firing shots around the rock-face.

A metallic smell stuck to the air, of gunpowder and the first trickles of blood. The gunfire echoed around the rock-face, rippling around their position like a thunderclap. Sixteen wiped his forehead and looked at the smoke dissipating into the sky.

Suddenly a whistle flew past Sixteen's left shoulder and a smaller puff appeared. The sound was granular. Another flew in front of him, sending a ball of dirt into his face. He wiped the dirt quickly from his eyes. Didshassi's head was buried in the sand; motionless, with blood pouring out of the side. He turned to where a finger was pointing.

The melee intensified, in slow motion. "To the west, you idiots. West! We are being flanked!" a voice screamed from behind. The fizz of bullets shattering rock and grenades clattering against the ground reverberated around Sixteen. Orange tints of barrels firing, and golden sparks of bullet casings glistened in his vision as the world around him became caked in high pitch wails.

Then mute. He finally squeezed the trigger, aiming at a figure with reddish clothing (like the desert itself) hiding behind the rat-a-tat-tat of rapid gunfire, two hundred yards away. His vision blurred in front of him. He adjusted his position and rested the barrel on a stone. He then closed his left eye and tried to line up the gunman in the crosshair of his rifle. It was an older man, not particularly tall, with a scraggly long beard of grey tendrils. The gunman gesticulated in Italian to the troops in his crosshair to move out of the way.

The arrow swayed, verging a wide arc. Sixteen controlled his breathing, closed both eyes, and thought about the mother whom he had never met. He then opened his right eye, squeezed the trigger, and let out a deep breath. His throat tasted of iron.

Sixteen awoke to the sound of Amiin groaning in his sleeping bag.

"What is it?" Sixteen said.

He looked at Amiin, shivering in the sleeping bag. Sweat

patches had made salt circles on his forehead. "Damn leg is giving me hell."

Sixteen could see a large brown stain that had seeped through to the outside of the sleeping bag.

He took a candle and moved next to Amiin. "Does it need re-bandaging?"

"Probably, but we don't have anything clean."

Sixteen unzipped his sleeping bag. "Let me see it," he said.

Amiin winced, the spacing between his eyebrows and hairline growing smaller with each wince.

"You must let me see it. Otherwise, you aren't going anywhere."

Amiin reluctantly nodded, the pain on his face leaking onto the floor.

He unzipped Amiin's trousers carefully, slowly unravelling the wounded leg caked in mud, dust, and blood. "Were these supposed to be green?" he laughed, unravelling the trouser leg.

The wound was halfway up the shinbone with lighter tinges around the edge. A trickle of bloody puss seeped from the mouth of the wound like a trickle of water snaking out of a dried-up stream. Amiin rummaged around in a rucksack, producing a small glass bottle. "Undo this cap will you."

Sixteen unscrewed the bottle. A strong acidic whiff blew into his nostrils as he passed the bottle back to Amiin. Amiin took a deep breath. "Here goes, kid!" he said, sprinkling drops of the clear liquid onto the wound. His left hand held a rock tight, while the wounded leg shivered uncontrollably.

"Can you move it?" Sixteen asked.

Amiin's right leg lay still, with the foot curling inwards. "Try again."

Amiin wheezed. He held his breath and tried to move the limb. "Any joy?" He looked at Sixteen in hopeful desperation. The foot and shin bone lay still.

He smiled at Amiin. "I'm sure it will be moving soon enough."

Amiin lay back on the sleeping bag. "Worthless piece of rubbish. Do not fail me now!" he screamed, tears streaming out of the corner of his eyes. "Please do not fail me now, Isra is close. I can feel it!"

He sat up, tapping the shin with a rolled-up newspaper. He tapped the leg harder. "JUST WORK!" he screamed. "BASTARD!" He hit the leg and howled like a mad dog. "Come! Come! Join us on this ride into the mystic lands where grapes grow and the Nile gushes crystal water. Where the blanket of clouds has departed, and the chaotic sound of songbirds fills the morning. Utopia it was once called. I will not scream anymore, just need you... what do you say... eh?"

Sixteen wiped his brow then loosened his shirt. Amiin's thrashed around on the floor, batting his limp leg with the newspaper. "WOOORRRKK!" he cried a final time before tossing the newspaper on the ground. He sobbed into his shirt sleeve, burying his face in the filthy linen.

Sixteen went over to the newspaper and picked it up off the ground; the paper ripped around the edges. He squinted at the faded ink, noticing the date ripped off the front page:

"CIVIL WAR PAUSES BETWEEN RIVAL FACTIONS"

Last night a ceasefire was declared in Somaliland, bringing an end to four years of fighting between the Goash militia and the Somali army. Somaliland, which has been at the forefront of the shale oil war has been torn apart during this period, with most of the population choosing to leave Somaliland, and becoming nomads of the desert.

Suspicion as to who had been supplying the two factions with weapons and artillery have included the Tarradeli family (from Italia), the Russia federation and the Oman/Saudi axis. Somaliland, for which has been ungoverned for years, had been seen as the final frontier of shale oil reserves when...

"Who taught you to read?" Amiin asked.

"Aleja. Did you know about this?" Sixteen replied.

"What is it?"

"Others funding the Goash and the Somali army?"

"Who are the Goash?"

"Our ancestors. Aleja taught us everything directly from their teachings and scriptures."

"More fundamentalists then… what else does it say?"

"About lands called Saud, Italy, Russia funding them."

Amiin turned away from Sixteen, focusing on a sharp piece of rock. "I heard lots of stories. Can you believe this was once a valuable piece of land? With prospectors from far away willing to invest in the salts of this dry earth."

Sixteen turned towards Amiin's back, where scratches lurked underneath the frayed shirt. "Invested? What does that mean?"

Amiin let out a raspy cough. "Means they show an interest. That is all."

"An interest?"

Amiin took a dirty piece of cloth from his trouser pocket "Yes, an interest. Listen, kid, tighten up this cloth for me, will you?" he said, breathing heavily.

"Just wrap it around?"

"Yes, just wrap it round the wound, quite tight. Didn't the great Aleja show you how to treat gunshot wounds?"

Sixteen nodded, dolefully. "He said to keep on fighting until the last breath is forced out of your lungs. The almighty one will treat you well in the afterlife."

Amiin shook his head. "Sounds like a big crock to me. What if these wounds CAN be treated?"

"Aleja said the wounds will heal in the next dimension. And not to fear as it wouldn't hurt."

"Try this for size!" He nodded at the useless limb. "Tie this cloth, no time to waste if I want to walk into the sunset, eh?"

A look of bewilderment crossed Sixteen's face. He picked up the faded cloth with two fingers, inspecting it from the underside. "Just tie it around the wound?" he asked.

Amiin nodded. "Just imagine it's like a big shoelace and my leg is the shoe. No need for bows, just a tight knot…" He tapped Sixteen on the back. "It's okay, you won't kill me, this old dog got some miles in him yet."

He thought about his age. Twenty-six years he had been treading the earth. He now felt tired and withered from his toils. But he also knew that his age was not old. Generations before him had lived passed fifty years old. *Fifty years – what an age!* he thought. *How lucky to not get an illness and find enough water and food to live so long.* He tried to pick up enthusiasm for the boy Sixteen, knowing his predicament was waning by the minute. For now, Isra felt far, far away. Like a boat slowing sailing from the shore.

Sixteen tied the cloth around the brittle shin bone. Mucus had congealed around the mouth of the wound. He winced as the dirty cloth touched the open wound, like he was feeling the pain, rather than Amiin.

Amiin bit down on his lip while his eyes flittered around the cave roof. "That will do, thank you."

Sixteen got to his feet and took three steps back. Amiin was a mess. Bones were sticking through his skin and a glacial shade filled his face. Ripple lines had emerged around his eyes; akin to sixty-year-old skin. He glanced at Amiin's receding hairline; the sweat and blood had given it a thickening oily quality, like a new-born baby.

Sixteen had a decision to make; leave or wither away like Amiin and Mak. Looking at the two he could see two stages of death staring him blankly in the face. *For what loyalty did he really have towards this prisoner? Aleja was gone so why was he helping him? Amiin was crippled and open to all the elements, disease, famine, dehydration, cannibalism.* He had seen the troops once devouring a human arm like a pack of hyenas fighting over a torn carcass.

He turned around to the land out of the cave entrance. Tugaar and Geed Hindi trees were dotted below the cave, their formations scattered amongst the patchy grass floor. The Tugaar trees foliage glistened against the sunlight, sliver in texture. The leaves spanned through the foliage like a huge spider-web, looking ever more delicate against the backdrop of the blue sky. He imagined falling out of the cave and landing on the pillowed branches softly. He then fixed on the ground, the rugged hard ground where despite the grasses a hard existence prevailed. Rocks of all shapes and sizes. That was all he knew, a grey land with splattering's of grassy green punctuated by concrete buildings and the occasional flicker of electric lights. This rolling scene would roll and roll until the ocean. He had heard many a tale but never seen it with his own eyes; of boats, waves, perfectly spherical rocks, creatures called crabs who lived on the shore. And the fish! He had always wanted to see a fish swimming. *Were they quick or slow? Did they have to come up for air? Was it cold down in the depths of the sea?*

"I'm tired…" said Amiin. "Real tired." He laid his head on a rolled-up jumper and closed his eyes. "You will have to go without me."

The light poured into the cave as Sixteen turned to face Amiin. "Go where?" he fiddled with the barrel of his rifle.

"Away from me. I can no longer walk."

"But where will I go? I am lost now."

"You are not lost. There is one person who can help us."

"Your sister?"

Amiin nodded, his gaze glazing over the cave ceiling. He took out a creased-up drawing from his trouser pocket. "Chances are she may not have seen the flare" – he coughed – "we have to try; you have to try, Sixteen."

He coughed again, spitting foamy mucus onto the cave ground. "This is her, years ago. She is a bit thinner now." With pain etched around his jowls he sat up. "I may have to beg."

Sixteen looked around the dry cave. At the rock formations that were millions of years old and the way the light and darkness clashed in certain corners. He then looked at Mak's body, discoloured and puffy lying in a corner where the darkness was devouring his spirit. He wiped his forehead and looked sternly at Amiin. He could feel the hairs at the back of his neck, erect. "Which direction?"

"Head west to the coast. Near the town of Hajidwali. Follow the coast from there."

"And if I find her?"

"You will find her."

"How do you know?"

"You will."

"There could be hundreds of Isras roaming the beaches."

Amiin grinned. "Ask her," he coughed violently. "Ask her what the juiciest side of a cooked beetle is." The smile beamed across his face at the mere thought of the response.

"Cooked beetle? Have you gone mad?"

Amiin composed himself, spitting blood on the floor. The smile refused to budge off his face, as brash and loud as the explosions they had witnessed.

"Ask her and you'll see."

Chapter Thirteen

Mary surveyed the crystalline morning sky, inhaling the fresher, cooler air.

She glanced over the flattened land where Socotra trees popped out of the rocky ground like mushrooms on a damp log. The red smoke faded behind a row of trees in the distance, leaving a trail of red dots.

"The coast. Has to be," said Mary.

"Don't think so. Think it's towards the hinterland," Isra replied.

"Coast, it looks to be from the northwest," Mary argued back.

Isra squinted her eyes: "No, it is south of the coast, where the grasses grow."

Isra threw her rucksack to the ground. Drawing an imaginary line with her finger she tried to plot a trajectory from where the red line of smoke could have originated. "It is the hinterland. Looks not too far from Hajidwali."

Mary released the rucksack from her shoulder and took out a water canister from the top pocket. She took a sip and flicked some water in her face. "Right now, a bit of breeze would be nice. Is that asking too much?"

She looked at the lines that had appeared over Isra's face. Indentations that had magically appeared one day along her forehead, cheeks, and chin. She could trace the lines back to the day they had left Mousa's body to rot. "What if it is Amiin?" Isra said, hoping.

"What if we are walking into an ambush?"

Isra took a dried-out piece of goat meat from her shirt pocket. The shirt dwarfed her slight frame. She nibbled on the meat, slowly munching in the corner of her mouth. "It fits the bill: the red colour, the rough location. IT HAS TO BE HIM!"

"Isra, are you sure it is a flare? Are we seeing things?"

"Close your eyes, take a deep breath and then tell me you can't see the red?"

Mary closed her eyes, counted to five, then opened them again.

"It's still there hanging in the air, isn't it?"

Mary sighed. "Appears to be. So, what now?"

A glint appeared in the corner of Isra's eye "It is Amiin. I can tell from the way it has lit up the sky. He is telling me something."

"How far do you think it is?"

"Twenty to thirty kilometres. We can get there by the morning sunrise."

"Tomorrow? What are you talking about! Have you seen our snail pace?"

Isra felt a jolt in her shoulder. She turned away from Mary. "Why all the negativity? This is not just for me. This is for you as well."

Mary looked on, an incredulous mask dwarfing her young face. "Couldn't fool me, Isra. Why is Amiin guiding us? He could be a bag of bones for all we know."

Isra glanced at the fading crumbs of red light dissipating from the distance. She felt a spirit also disappearing into the atmosphere. A tear dropped from her cheek. "Don't say that!"

"Why? It could be true. I'm just being realistic is all."

"My you've grown up quickly."

"What do you mean?"

"You're acting too much like the adult nowadays."

Mary's brow crossed. She kicked some stones on the ground. "How else am I supposed to act? Just you and me now."

Isra started to feel guilty about Mousa. A feeling that came and went but was constantly chipping away in the background. *Did Mary secretly blame her for Mousa's demise? Mary had changed, gone were the doleful expressions and naïve comments when she was enslaved. Now all that was left was cold, hard facts turned into calculated survival options.*

Mary eventually yielded to Isra's wish. They followed the road towards Hajidwali that led into the hinterland, the same path Isra had trodden as a toddler with Amiin years previously.

On either side of the road the hills started to smoothen out as they progressed side by side, hand in hand taking shelter from the sunshine under tall Qudac Acacia trees that hung lopsided over the gravel path like a wicked, shrub canopy. It had taken only a couple of kilometres for the landscape to change; the air had a freshness to it, like the smell of grasses growing after heavy rainfall. The barren rocky wilderness was giving way to flat, fertile, green patches that appeared to swallow up the rocks.

Mary took a water canister from a clip on her belt and shook it. "Looks like I'm out. Do you have any?"

Isra nodded. "Few drops, might need to take a detour."

"Another detour? Can't we just get there? Can't be that far, can we?"

"Twelve, fifteen kilometres, but we aren't going far without water."

"So where can we get water?"

Isra shifted her rucksack around her shoulders, looking past the ridge. "Let me think. Sure, there was a well near here."

Mary sighed, turning her back to Isra. Her body suddenly buckled, collapsing to the ground.

"Mary!" cried Isra.

Isra threw the rucksack to the ground and ran over to Mary's slumped body, down in the dirt. "Mary! Are you okay? Say something!" She shook Mary's back, hoping to coax a pinch of life out of her. That feeling of dread fizzed around her veins yet again, of loss, pain, loneliness. For a split second she imagined what it would be like to lose Mary. It was like a spear impaling her heart. She grabbed Mary's shirt and turned her over.

Mary's hair covered her eyes, with soil clinging to her milky cheeks. Her lips quivered. "Gotcha!" she sat up.

A glaze haunted Isra's eyes, like she had seen the resurrection. "Don't do that!"

Mary rolled to one side and jumped to her feet, a broad grin lighting up her face. She laughed aloud, for all the desert to hear. "Had you there, Isra! Had you there!"

Isra looked to one side. She was right, Mary had her. Because for that one moment she felt the emotions most associated with letting go. The same emotions when she had left Amiin, and the same emotions he must have felt when he had left their mother on the beach. Relief started to trickle into her veins, flushing out the fear. She turned to Mary, all giddy, child-like. Her childhood was still there, manifested in a play dead game that she once played with Amiin. Her lips parted and a smile appeared while the sun brushed past another cloud.

"See, you are laughing!" said Mary. "The stone queen smiles. Rejoice!"

And she chuckled; again, and again. "Don't do that!" she stood up, trying to conceal the laughter ripples.

"Last time I can act dead you know."

Isra wiped her eyes with her shirt sleeve. "How do you mean?"

"Next time it will be for real."

The tears were still wet under her eyes. "Don't say that!"

"It is true. Only have one more chapter, next one is death." She shook her head, dropping the tears of laughter to the ground where they would quickly dry up.

"Enough of this, we must find the well."

Mary looked around. "So where is it?"

She pointed forwards. "This road leads to the Hajidwali dwelling. It is hiding under a red stone with a mark on it."

"What kind of mark?"

Isra formed her fingers together, forming a diamond pattern. "Like this."

Mary knelt, her breath shallow. "Who lives in the Hajidwali dwelling?"

"Could be anyone now. When we passed it was a family

of three. Man, and two children from what I remember. Very young they were."

"Where was the mother?"

"They'd left her in a town somewhere in the Ethiopian desert, from what I remember."

"Why did they leave her?"

"Was invaded by a bandit troop that came from the Sahara."

Mary kicked a rock towards a large Acacia in front. The stones rebounded off the bark into a patch of grass beneath. "Why'd they leave her?"

"I was young. Cannot remember."

"Try and remember," Mary pressed.

"Probably sick, isn't that why you would leave somebody? Anyway, let's go. Will be night in a few hours, and we need to get near the well. I'm getting thirsty answering all your questions."

"We can walk and talk."

Isra wiped her mouth with her shirt sleeve. Barely an ounce of moisture stained her shirt. Her vision swayed gently from side to side, like a metronome. Mary stood upright in front of her, with rucksack on ready to go. "What are we waiting for?"

Isra bent down and grabbed at the rucksack which seemed far away. She extended her arm again.

"Here…" Mary picked the rucksack up and looped the straps around Isra's shoulders. "Just point in the right direction. Let's talk once we've found the well."

Mary's outline was wavy, crisscrossing between ground and sky. Her hair blew gently against a breeze, longer and thicker than moments before.

The rucksack was thrown onto her shoulders, and she instantly felt the weight. This time it felt heavier, like the rucksack was leaden with desert boulders. Her thighs stung, the pain moving into her hipbones. It was then she felt the old adage of the weight of the world, their own existences on her very shoulders. She buried her emotions deep into the pit of her stomach and moved slowly, one foot in front of the other.

The hours melted into the fading sunshine and every step was harder for Isra. The pain commuted around her body, from the soles of her feet right to the tip of her cranium. Mary pushed Isra along.

Twilight approached when the silver outline of Hajidwali's buildings could be seen.

"There, I can see it," Isra hushed.

Mary stopped pushing and appeared by the side. She now appeared as her usual appearance; shorter, with a slighter frame and a sticky mess of hair flopping against the side of her face. "The well?"

"I can see Hajidwali. The outline of the buildings."

Mary moved her neck to the side. "We don't need to go into the town, do we?"

"We will need to get near the outskirts, so I can get my bearings. The dark is going to help us, though."

Blotchy violet lines Mary could see in the sky, blending into a covering of slate weaving between the clouds. The tendrils thickened and thinned out, flowing like rivers into the universe.

Stars started to arise beyond the mesh of tangled colours, clearer than she had seen for a long time. She felt a warmth from the stars, out there in a galaxy lightyears away. Her lips parted. "Anyone be annoyed if we stray into the town?" she said.

"Let's hope not."

"Who was passing through?"

"Tribes crossing from the Sahara I was told. White folk with long beards, their families, washed up on the coast. I don't remember a lot of hostility from them, unless Amiin didn't tell me."

Their footsteps scrunched against the loose stones on the floor. Isra opened her mouth and released her tongue into the air, hoping for moisture in the baked air. Her trouser leg dragged along the ground, covering the sandals on her feet.

As she bent down to tie the trouser leg into a knot she fell backwards, her rucksack cushioning the fall.

"Can't, caaaan't tieee tie this leg around shoe, sandal, shoooooeee." Her head sunk backwards into the cushioned part of the rucksack. "T... tt... tie it willllll you?" she murmured towards the tendrils in the sky.

"No point," said Mary bluntly.

Isra gazed at the sky, her eyelids shuttering in and out. "Huh?"

"There is no point."

"Whaat, whaaat you mean?"

Mary crouched next to Isra. "Is pretty clear, Isra. I need to get the water. You can't go any further."

"Nooo stop being, stooooop being ridiculous."

"You said it was to the left of the town, right? A hundred yards or so?"

Isra shook her head.

"Okay, here is what we're going to do. I need you to point roughly where this well is. Then I need you to keep your eyes open, do not drift off. I'll wrap you in some blankets to keep warm, but you must keep your eyes open while I'm gone, okay?"

"I.... caaaan I caaaannn go."

Mary swept Isra's fringe away from her eyes and cradled her chin in the palm of her hand. "Isra, you have done enough. I can handle this, be just like another trip to another town. Like it was with Mousa. Yes?"

Isra nodded. She grabbed Mary by the arm. "Run if you see trouble. Ruuuuun," she whispered.

Mary took out two plastic bottles from her rucksack and one out of the side of Isra's rucksack. She threw her rucksack to the ground and puffed out her shoulders. "Right where does the adventure lead me?"

Isra turned her head to the left. "There's a... there's aaa tall metal thing, shaped like... shaaaaped like a lizard's... a liz... lizard's head. Heeeaad wessst down, down a hill it...

it… flaaaaatens and it's… it'sssssss there," she coughed, pointing in the general direction.

Mary tossed a blanket out of her rucksack and wrapped it around Isra's shoulders. "I won't be long. Remember to stay awake, count flies or something."

She got to her feet, with bottles to hand. "Mary," Isra had a shiver in her voice.

"Yes."

"Whaaat beans have you…" she paused for breath "… have you been eating?"

"Beans?"

"Beans… beeeans of courage, Mary!"

Mary glanced at Isra, a steely determination emanating from her face. "I'm eating the same tasteless crap as you, Isra." She crunched the bottles with her hands.

Isra could see Mary's silhouette in the moonlight, running towards the dimmed light of crumpled buildings that stood like decrepit monoliths about to fall. A hyena call echoed from the east, wailing into the night like a call to prayer. She was suddenly drawn to a green light on top one of the buildings, flashing from side to side. She scrunched her eyes up to fight the hallucinations. It was still there. She threw her head back and vomited. After the final drip had left her mouth she looked up to the starry heavens and prayed for Mary. She had not prayed for a long, long time. And there was no god that she worshipped.

Chapter Fourteen

Mary caught sight of the verdant light juddering from the roof-top in front of her. Using the moonlight, she stepped forward carefully, following the natural contours downhill into a small ditch. In the ditch the moonlight failed, plunging her into darkness. She felt around the side of the rocks and pushed herself back over the side of the rock wall where the green light was visible, a short distance away.

"Damn thing where is it?" she mumbled. In front she could see the outline of the buildings and a vast blackness underneath. She looked down the hill where the pit was darkest, over the rock wall and back towards the reference point of the green light; nothing. She could barely make out her hand placed in front. All she could see from the moonlight was the shadowy buildings and the outline of the wall in front.

The green dot then appeared to focus on a specific area, scanning a tightened circle beneath. She moved up the hill towards the building, carefully treading where she could see a clearer path that was not filled with rocks or rubbish. The path led to the left side of the building. She tip-toed uphill around the perimeter, concentrating on the position of the green dot. A muffled sound of voices suddenly rose out of the building. She stopped, ducking under the wall. The muffle grew ever so louder, she could hear traces of Arabic, Italian. She scanned the darkness, looking for the metal lizard's head shining against the moonlight while the muffled chat weaved in and out. The top of the structure then poked out in the distance behind the back of the building. She could make out a shiny slab. It looked more like a giant egg than a lizard's head, hiding between her view of the wall and the back of the building.

A dense oily smell clung to her nostrils as she drew closer to the building. She quickly jumped over the wall and looked up at the green dot. A lump formed in her throat. She then realised she was on her own and that there was nobody to bail her out. She took a deep breath and moved forward, feeling inside her pocket for the knife she had slain Mousa with. Half of Mousa's face appeared in front of her: "*You are nothing without me!*" he said, snarky.

She moved towards the metal egg, trying to see the best place to navigate down the hill but the lack of moonlight was inhibiting her progress. Also, the ground was becoming wetter; she could feel her feet slipping on the ground as the smell of oil intensified.

The voices came and went, like whispers in the wind. She was a few yards from the building but no closer to the metal egg. To her left was a black hole, devoid of moonlight so she continued to follow the moonlight towards the metal egg; all the while keeping a close eye on the green dot that felt like it was watching her. She skirted around the perimeter of the building, around bricks scattered on the ground until a path of gravel shone against the moonlight. She quickly headed for the scatterings of gravel, dimly lit against the moonlight. A crunch then frightened her. She looked at the ground. It was a glass bottle she had stepped on. The sound immediately seemed to awaken the drifting voices into a chagrin, uniformed array of shouts. The green dot moved towards her precarious position.

She ran blindly towards the gravel path, tripping over the loose rubbish. Behind she could hear the clamber of men mobilising as the green light extinguished from the roof. It was the same shouts and scuffs of boots on gravel, the familiar tangy odour of worn shirts and stale breath. It was men, running towards her but she could not see them. She got to her feet and followed the loose flow of gravel where the path faded down the hill into a blind pit. The moonlight poked through cracks in the trees and bushes that lined the path. Taking one step discreetly at a time she stepped forward, hoping for the well to appear. She sniffed the air for the scent of the men. They were close. Waving the bottles in front she slowly stepped forward until a concrete slab collided with her knee.

She felt around the slab, barely noticing the pain. The slab was up to her waist, icy cold. An abrasive texture like a worn piece of rope brushed her fingers. She tugged at the rope, which was torqued tight, dropping the plastic bottles to the ground. Up the hill the green dot now appeared, and a racket of voices followed. She tugged at the rope again, and again, leaning back on her heels. The rope became heavier. She dug her feet into the ground and pulled again. She pulled harder while the green light shone brighter, descending the hill. A clattering sound emerged from within the slab, she touched the top of the slab, feeling a plastic rim. Her hands dived inside the rim. *It was water!* She felt around the rim, cupped her hands together and took a mouthful. The cooling taste rushed through the ulcers of her tongue and to the back of her throat. It was a taste of wonder. She stuck her head in the bucket and gulped a large mouthful. The cooling sensation on her face was like a breeze in the desert on a parched day. She grinned broadly at a star, thankful.

The muffled voices grew louder, echoing and rebounding down the hill like a rowdy conversation of demented, evil spirits. She sensed they were close. Feeling on the ground for the bottles she inflated them by blowing through the nozzle and filled them in the bucket. Once they were filled, she could not resist the urge to take another mouthful. As she surfaced from the bucket the green light flashed in front of her. She dashed behind a tree to the side, clutching the bottles for dear life.

"Che era finite li."

"Dove!"

The outline of two figures appeared out of the fading moonlight. One significantly shorter than the other, wearing a cap. The green light wavered from side to side. Mary glanced at the light that wobbled between the trees and the path, the outline of a rifle butt just visible.

"Deve essere ben."

The voices sounded remarkably similar, like one person talking. The light flickered, drawing closer as her heartbeat raced under her jacket, pumping a distress signal to Isra.

"Controllare lagiu."

She could see where the green dot was heading, on top of her position. She clutched the two bottles tightly and ran away from the well, further down the pitch-black hill. A rancid smell gripped her, the further she delved into the darkness, a strange concoction of chemicals, latrines.

"Eh! Chi e quello!! Chi e quello!!"

The crack of gunfire echoed around her ears. One, two, three shots that went from left to right ear, ping-ponging inside her head like marbles clattering against her inner skull. She ran as fast as she could into a blind tunnel. A new instinct took hold, an instinct of awareness she had not felt before. An instinct that guided her feet away from the many obstacles that lay on the damp ground, and away from the tree stumps and gunfire. It felt like her feet were gliding just above the ground, away from the dangers ahead. She looked up at the star shining brighter, who had followed her from the edge of the town.

"Bastardo tornare! Tornare!" the smooth voice weakened. "Toooorrrrrnare!"

A final round of gunfire crackled her left ear before she lost her footing and tumbled into a ditch. The voices passed above her and continued haphazardly down the hill, the green dot fading into the tangled web of trees. She stood, suddenly realising that the bottles were out of her grasp.

"Gah!" she sighed, omitting a puff of vapour into the night. She felt her left knee, it was sore where she had landed. She bent down, feeling around the mud until the bottle connected with the tips of her hand. She picked up the bottle, leaving it with two hands to her left position. With her right hand she scanned the ground. Small stones scraped against her fingertips, intermingled with the acrid sludge. She tried to picture the sludge in her hands; lumpy, chestnut in colour, rolling out of her hands ever so slowly.

A sharp pain suddenly caught her right thumb. She jilted her wrist away from the ground, it felt like blood. She wiped it on her jacket, took a sip of the water-bottle near her feet and scanned the ground for the other bottle. A panic gripped her tight within her chest, a panic like no other she had felt; not even when the knife blade had plunged into Mousa's back or when she had fought off the bandits who tried to rob her of her virginity. Her hands hurriedly scraped against the sludgy ground, scraping against sharp rocks and glass for the other bottle. The panic grew faster in her chest, a resounding tightening of the blood vessels that brought her lungs together. Her breath was shallow, like one long breath that would never end as the black wall pressed in against her face, smothering her existence into the mud. Then the crinkled plastic grazed her bloodied fingertips; it was faint but there, somewhere. She went back to the same spot carefully until the bottle was within her grasp. She gripped the bottle top tightly, but it was lodged in the ground. She pulled harder with both hands until the bottle came loose from the mud; and she cradled the bottle in her hands like a new-born baby, with relief sweating through the pores of her forehead. She grabbed the other bottle and collapsed on the ground. In her blurred vision the star winked through the outlines of dry leaves on the trees. It was Isra, she could feel her embracing gaze.

She then retraced her steps up the hill; one hand waving in front of the other whilst clutching the bottles tightly, one foot scanning the ground in front of the other. Fluorescent outlines of creatures appeared in front, as large as her fist. Some creatures flew, others scurried on the ground. Shape-shifting from puffy round to long and worm-like. Her head shook as the creatures faded into the darkness.

The ground hardened as the acrid smell passed the further she ascended the hill. The moonlight slowly left a trail of nickel grey around the outline of the giant egg and her sight started to return, trees, boulders, her own hands. The wall appeared and she jumped over it quickly. After a detour around the perimeter of the building she eventually found Isra curled up like a bug, hibernating in the crack of a tree trunk.

She leant down and shook Isra by the shoulder. "Here, drink," she said.

Isra's eyes were closed, her feet twitching.

She shook Isra again "Wake up… I said stay awake!"

Isra's eyes opened, circumspect. Mary glanced at Isra's face; she looked to have aged in the few hours she had been away.

She unscrewed the bottle top and placed the mouth of the bottle gently towards Isra's lips. Isra gasped at the water, clutching at the bottle fiercely. Mary glanced into the sky, looking for the star but nothing could be seen — a grouping of clouds was beginning to form over Hajidwali. Isra placed the bottle on the ground. "What took you so long?"

Mary looked away from the sky, a faint whiff of oil passed through her nose. "Ran into a bit of trouble. Didn't you hear?"

"Hear what?"

"Doesn't matter."

"What was it?

"Nothing I cannot handle. Mission accomplished right?"

Isra nodded, looking concerned.

Mary took a sip of the water. "How are you feeling?"

"Better after that sleep."

"So, you did. I told you not to! What if you had gone all unconscious on me?"

Isra batted her hand into the air, haughtily.

Mary looked again at the sky. Light silver specks were peeking through the clouds, she turned towards the buildings of Hajidwali. The building tops were clearer, and beyond she could almost make out the sheen of the giant egg. The first signs of dawn were approaching.

"We've got to get going, it's not safe around here," said Mary.

"Why, what's going on in the town?"

"I don't know it was pitch black, but there were some awful smells coming from there."

"What kind of smells?"

"Oil, sewage I'm not sure. Was yucky."

She passed the bottle to Isra. "Who did you have trouble with back there?"

"Didn't see them, just heard them. Italian, I think."

A pensive look graced Isra's face, like she had seen a ghost. "Italian?"

"Think so. One of the European languages."

Isra sipped on the water, taking small gulps. "We had better move on. Not far to go now."

Mary looked again at the fading night sky. "I hope so, Isra. I am getting sick and tired of all this moving. I need to stop somewhere and rest."

Isra threw the blanket to one side and got to her feet. She then picked the rucksack up. "This is the last time I am sticking this thing on my back. I promise you."

"Are we still heading inland?"

"I had a dream; Amiin was on the beach. I think we need to head back that way."

Mary smiled wryly. She felt tired but seeing Isra regenerate gave her strength. Strength and hope that she had someone looking out for her. Someone who would not hit her unnecessarily across the face, would not speak down to her like vermin or let starve in the baking heat. Isra was not Mousa. They both held hands for a second, looked to the new dawn approaching and continued towards the beaches, knowing that aspirations would be reset soon, for this journey they had taken was about to end. Their lives would change irrevocably, one way or another and Mary hoped secretly that Isra wanted to be part of it. For this was a future that she was starting to dream about.

Chapter Fifteen

Sixteen set his rucksack on the ground, breathing in the salty air that tickled the back of his throat. He wiped his brow with the corner of his jumper sleeve, sitting down on the rocks. *So, this is it. The coast. The end of the land*, he thought.

He had dreamed about this moment throughout adolescence; the waves, the wet sand, the turquoise sea lapping up the clouds in the sky until the line blurred between the horizons. He walked onto the beach, scooping the water into his hands.

"Don't drink it," Amiin had advised Sixteen. "Will make you sick." The water had a different texture to the scraps of liquid in the hinterland. It was finer, gliding through his fingers like fine silk.

The temptation to drink the water was tempting; he wiped his lips, the salty air exacerbating the thirst. *What rubbish! A wall of water, I am dying for a drink and now I can't drink the damn stuff!* He knew the almighty one in the clouds was evaluating him. Amiin then popped into his mind, lying in the cave helpless, in pain. He hoped his heart was still beating and that his mind was clear.

He scanned the beach. Gulls glided along the coast, singing to each other. He walked back over the tidal sands to pick up his rucksack. He looked around at the panorama of sea, clouds, and sand; not a soul was in sight.

Rusty cooking pans, plastic bottles filled with algae, butane canisters littered the beach. Blending into the scene like the rocks of the hinterland. Small rectangular shapes shining in the daylight.

He had heard stories. Small boxes, made of minerals dug out of the ground. The boxes communicated with each other; although he could not make out how. Aleja had proclaimed one day, *"These little devices were sent from hell first class, to pollute the minds of our species."* Aleja adamantly believed that this land, with its minerals, had once been the battleground. Sixteen looked at the cracked glass screens and rusted metal casing, dumbfounded.

"Move along the coast westbound, looping the sandy beach and the rocky cliffs until you find her," Amiin had instructed Sixteen. He clutched at the photograph, admiring the pearl beauty of Isra's eyes, the rusty complexion covering her skin. Her wavy hair was tied into a tight ponytail, showing her high boned cheeks.

He placed his palm over his forehead and scanned the beach eastbound, in the direction he had come from "Hello! Yo! Yo!" he shouted. He could feel his voice disintegrating into the vastness of the ocean to his left and the desert to the right.

The beach looked endless, like one yellow line snaking along the cliffs. He looked down at the waves and the tide, an ongoing battle between land and water. Aleja had taught him about creation and man's place. The almighty one had given the order to reclaim the land one fine day, and thus life walked out of the ocean. A giant horde of sharks that could suddenly stand upright and talk. Then came the evolution from fish to man. Sixteen scratched his head, perplexed at nature and the order of evolution.

The clouds gathered along the horizon, blotting out the blueness. "Hello! Hello!" he shouted again. In the near distance a red speck drifted in between the two clouds. He had seen a similar speck inland whilst patrolling, like a red cloud that would not disappear. *Was it a sign?* The last time a red spot appeared in the sky Aleja's group had befallen to an attack.

Being around Amiin had given him a comfort blanket that a gunfight was no big deal, just another chapter in living like cutting your toenails or combing your hair. But now amongst the calming sea-winds and faint call of the gulls he felt a clarity. He was lucky to be alive.

He wiped his bleeding nose on his sleeve, turned around and headed up a small cliff for his next loop; knowing time was running out to get back to Amiin. He leant down, grabbing a clump of grass nestled between the cliff rocks and chewed on the clump. The hunger pains were kicking in again, like a draining force eating up his intestines. Energy was sapping out of his body by the minute. He could see visions of a watery mess sweating out of his armpits and onto the ground. *When will this end?* All he wanted right now was a cold drink and a nice chunk of meat to gnaw on. He sat on the grassy patch, crestfallen. The gulls cawed in the distance as he closed his eyes; hearing the lapping of silky waves onto the carpeted beach intertwined with the shrill cawing. He could feel his body drifting into a dream. Suddenly a voice drifted along the beach into his consciousness. It was the deft tone of a girl, shouting.

He opened his eyes, looking to the bottom of the cliff to where the voice was originating. He looked at the beach, then to the winding coastal strip eastbound. There he saw the faint images of two figures, heading in his direction. He ducked down and lay on the ground. *Was it her? Was it Isra? The Ilhama of Amiin?* He poked his eyes through the prism of a toppled tree trunk, noticing two figures carrying heavy rucksacks; one with a cap, the other had long hair blowing in the wind. They were wandering aimlessly along the beach, as if the wind were about to take them both out to sea.

The walking style was languid, crisscrossing along the beach like ghostly dogs. He winked several times to shake off the illusions, then waved at the two figures.

"Hey! Hey!"

The outline of the figures became clearer. The one with the cap seemed to be leading the way.

"Hey!" he shouted again. This time the figure with the cap looked up. It looked like a female. Her skin radiated against the sliver of sunshine poking through the clouds; tender and bronzed. She took her cap off and waved it towards Sixteen. Her hair was chocolate brown, cut short. Sixteen motioned to the beach, indicating a rendezvous, and made his way carefully down the rock-face.

As his feet touched the sand the girl approached him. He awaited apprehensively, assuming it was Isra. Pensively she stopped twenty feet from Sixteen, looking behind.

"You are?" she said.

Sixteen noticed scars on her forearms that glowed. "Does it matter?"

"Of course it matters. Who are you?"

Sixteen smirked, looking to the sea "Attitude I see."

"Attitude... I like to think of it as caution."

"From what?"

"Never you mind. It's done me well so far."

Her companion drew close. Sixteen glanced at her immaculate frizzy hair flopping over her ears. He knew then it was Isra.

"You will have to tell us your name," said Isra, coughing.

"I'm not here to harm you," he replied.

"Isra, my name is Isra. And this is my companion, Mary. There you go."

Sixteen focused solely on Isra, drawn to the aquamarine glints in her eyes that danced off the waves. "So, you are Isra. Thank the almighty one I have found you."

Isra turned to Mary, befuddlement stretched their thin faces. "Do I know you?" she asked.

"No, you don't know me."

Their voices muted, punctuated by the tide creeping onto the beach. "What side... what side do you like the beetle to be cooked on?" he said.

Mary shook her head. "What are you talking about, stranger?"

Isra's face suddenly lit up. The grey, charred tone that was suffocating the effervescence underneath dissipated into the ocean. The glints turned to flashes as her eyes widened, for all the world to see. Sixteen looked on, transfixed by her face opening like the breaking of dawn.

"Amiin… you have seen him? Where is he?" Tears rolled down her cheeks.

Mary ran at Sixteen, holding the knife out in front. "Where is he? What have you done to him?" she screamed, grabbing Sixteen by the collar and holding the knife to his neck.

"Hold up, girl, hold up. Let me explain."

"Speak!"

Sixteen fixed on to Isra. A look of panic was now gripping her face tightly. "Amiin was captured by our group."

Mary lowered the blade. "What group?"

"Led by the prophet called Aleja, who believed the almighty one had sent him to earth. He was our saviour." Sixteen wiped his brow.

"We wandered and wandered as a group, a group of orphan boys. Scared to leave Aleja for he gave us all a purpose, a goal. We were battling for our god. Our god who would look after us in heaven. We wandered until one day a firefight broke out with another group. There were many injuries, deaths."

"Who were the other group?"

"I am not sure. They had fair skin and talked in the Euro languages. Amiin and I escaped, ending up in a cave near to here. He fired a flare to give you a signal."

"Where is he?" Isra asked.

"Still there. He asked me to come and find you."

Mary brought the blade up to Sixteen's chin "But why is he not with you? You better not be ambushing us!"

Sixteen grinned. "Ambush? I am too tired for all that. Do you have any water?"

"Answer the question!"

"He's still in the cave, nursing a wound."

"Wound? How bad?" said Isra.

"Gunshot wound to the leg. He cannot walk on it."

Isra took a bottle from the side pouch of her rucksack, handing it to Sixteen. Sixteen grabbed at the bottle, gulping at the water ferociously. "He gave me this," he handed the photograph to Isra.

Isra held the photograph against the sunlight, barely recognising the innocent girl imprinted on the paper. "Is that me?"

Sixteen nodded.

Mary took a step away from Sixteen. "What's your name?"

"Call me Sixteen."

"Funny name."

"Only one I know."

"Sixteen lives… like a cat has nine?"

Sixteen smiled, taking another sip of water. He could see Mary's hard exterior starting to melt. "It's what Aleja called me."

"How far is this cave?" said Isra.

"Took me just over eight hours without stopping. It's into the hinterland, just before the desert opens up."

"And this other group, the Europeans you say. Are they close?"

"That, I don't know."

Isra nodded to Mary. They stepped to one side.

Mary twiddled with the lace on her shirt. "I don't like the sound of this. Chances are it's the same bunch I ran into at Hajidwali."

"Could be, but what is the chance we will run into them again? Who knows what they want?"

"Feels safer here that is all. We would be going back on ourselves into that dried up hole inland."

Isra held Mary by the hand, a sign of resignation in her eyes. "Mary, I must go. I would rather die trying to find Amiin than staying here. I am sorry."

Mary knew deep down that resistance to this latest foray would be futile. Isra's eyes pierced deep into her retinas, without blinking. The colours changing and absorbing one another into a kaleidoscope that sparkled intensely. It was like staring into the sun unabated.

"Do you trust this *Sixteen lives*?"

"I do."

"How?"

"He knows Amiin. I am certain."

Mary took a step away, throwing the blade on the sand. Pulling her hands over her eyes she groaned. It would be more footsteps in the baking heat; more blisters on her feet and more sweat drops draining the life out of her body. But she owed it to Isra. There was no other option. "Can we come back here eventually? It seems nice and peaceful."

Isra winked at Mary. "Let us see."

They rested a few minutes, lapping up the fresh sea air before moving back onto the long, treacherous road with Sixteen. Their progress was slow; hampered by blustery winds coming in from the desert blowing up thick dust clouds. They scuttled along the hollow roads, tasting grit and shielding their eyes from the hellish winds that whistled against the boulders and the cacti. Dusk approached with barely a blink of an eye, bringing a calm breeze that brushed off the surface of the rocks. They drank their water sparingly and nibbled at rations of leaves, mud, and bone marrow.

Isra trailed behind the others, breathing heavily. The more she dragged her feet along the ground the more energy sapped out of her pores, creating deep sores around her ankles.

Sixteen turned around. "Are you okay?"

Isra nodded.

"Let me take your bag," he said.

"I am fine. Just keep going."

"Not the answer I was looking for!" Sixteen grappled at Isra's shoulders until the rucksack broke loose. She had barely any fight to stop him.

"I want that back once we reach my brother."

"You're the boss!"

Mary turned around, wiping her brow with her sleeve. "Likes to think she is," she said.

"When did I say that?"

"Isra, you think you are, that's true. Only one boss and he is up there somewhere. He has a plan."

"Since when did you start believing?"

"I've just been thinking about it."

"Well, instead of thinking about gods and great plans, let us hurry. Don't want to be stranded in the cold."

Isra could sense Amiin was close. There was something in the air; a kind of sweet scent that grew stronger as the night closed in. It was then that her heart began to race a thousand beats in her chest. *What would she say to him? How would she explain the Mousa incident? What if Sixteen was leading them all into an ambush?* Her instinct grew stronger with every step. And now it was saying continue, despite her withering body giving way. The more she continued down the dusty road the more her mother's voice whispered into her ear. *"Get to Amiin! Hurry, Isra! Hurry!"* Her legs, filled with cramps and blisters marched past Sixteen and Mary.

"How far, Sixteen?" she shouted with back turned.

"Another kilometre, I think."

Sixteen took a deep breath, he could taste wood burning on his tongue. Dried up twigs emerged either side of the dusty brown earth, forming a hedged barrier around the path that began the climb into the hills. He looked down at tiny spots of moss; the only remnants of green foliage from the ground, taken over by the barren, beige carpet that Isra and Mary thought they had escaped. Sixteen picked up a handful of the fine, crumbed earth. He felt the texture and blew it off his hand. *No wonder the crops had failed for so long,* he thought. *Even a blade of grass would struggle to survive in this.*

The mating calls of hyenas filled the air; sharp shrieks that rattled Sixteen's eardrums. He had heard them before in the hinterland but never this loud. The shrieks attacked his temple with a sledgehammer, conjuring images of devil children the further they progressed up the hill. The black hole in the cave was within sight. *Were the mating calls a signal for something else?* He was eager to see Amiin again.

Sixteen pointed to the top of the hill. "Just up there."

The faint moon peeped out behind a cloud on their final leg, guiding them towards the cave.

The hyena cackles faded. Isra tepidly put one foot in front

of the other like she was skipping along cracking ice. Her heart thumped uncontrollably, reverberating into the twilight where her mother sat watchfully on a cloud. The mouth of the cave came into view; a dark abyss that looked like a vortex carved into the crumbling stone. "Amiin! Brother!" she shouted. "Amiin!"

She turned the corner into the cave, her naked destiny displayed. His feet were facing outward, stretched in perfect angles either side. She approached his face where the moonlight shone ever so slightly, glazed onto his retinas like a heavenly tattoo.

Her heartbeat stopped for a second, the coldness of the cave shook her bones, enclosing her being while she stared longingly at the shell of body in the darkness. No maggots or jackals hacking at the corpse. The finality lay before her. Mary put her hand on Isra's shoulder while a solitary tear fell on the cave floor. This was Amiin, her dead brother. And her mother's face disappeared into the night.

Chapter *Sixteen*

"I'm sorry, Isra."

The word sorry. What did it mean? Sorry for what? This strange word mentioned many times in the days after Amiin's death. *Sorry was something you said when you said something nasty to somebody or hurt them. Why were they sorry?* Sixteen or Mary had not put Amiin to the sword. Mary had not even said sorry to Isra when the dagger went into Mousa's back. This was now a strange, strange world she viewed when the sun rose, and the night came.

They buried Amiin in the morning. The earth was sandy enough to dig a hole with relative ease in the ground below the cave. They chose a spot next to a dead palm tree further down the hillside, a spot of no real significance; just another spot of dried-up land that the sun and the wind had chewed up over the years.

Sixteen knew of a well nearby so they filled their guts with water and set about digging. They had no shovels so improvised with sticks and tent-poles until the earth was just deep enough to bury the body.

Both Sixteen and Isra wrapped Amiin in a ragged piece of silk cloth that barely covered his torso and slowly lowered the corpse into the ground. Isra looked down, transfixed at the ghost that lay hapless before her. She could see his gut expanding like a bulb on a cactus. His skin was ash coloured, with white flecks dotted around the cheeks. She took a deep breath, with tears holed up. *Was this a goodbye? It did not feel like it.* She laid a hand on his stone-cold chest, imagining it beating in another galaxy beyond her dreams.

With a nod to Sixteen the hole filled with the red earth. Her final image of Amiin, her brother, was the subtlest of grin's poking out of the side of his mouth as the earth filled around his ears.

"Are you okay?" Sixteen asked.

Isra suddenly felt dizzy, lost. She fell to the ground, staring at the patch of ground where his corpse lay. Soon the corpse would be fresh gain for the worms, scorpions, jackals, hyenas, vultures. The soul, once clinging to the tissue of Amiin's body would soon move to the next realm.

Sixteen knelt and held Isra tight. He could hear sobs of anguish. She reciprocated with the faintest of embraces.

"If it wasn't for him, I would never have escaped Mousa," said Mary.

Sixteen let Isra go. "He led me out of the chaos," he said.

Isra wiped her face with her shirt sleeve "How... how did he die? I thought he was going to make it," she said bluntly.

"I... I do not know, Isra. I am as shocked as you. He was in pain with his leg. We bandaged it tight."

"Did you have antiseptics?"

"I... I... I don't think so. We weren't able to get any I was... was going to... going to try and... and... pick some up." Sixteen's voice quivered. He relayed back the last conversation with Amiin, but all he could recall was a blurred mix of platitudes, instructions. It did not feel like the final goodbye.

"How did you get out of the firefight to the cave?" Mary asked.

"I took the bags. He used two sticks to hobble along."

"So, you managed to sneak out without being detected. Even though Amiin had been shot?"

"Yes, he asked for my help. Please believe me."

"And what were his last words then, eh?"

Sixteen sat down, scraping the sides of his head with his fingers. Guilt was clawing away at his insides. *Why did you leave him? You knew he was paralysed. Wrong choice. He would never have died had you stayed.* "He was just talking about you, Isra. That was his only concern. To see you and make sure you were safe."

Isra turned away from the grave. She lent down, wrapping a scarf around her neck, kicking gravel into the grave. "We need to make sure the animals don't dig him up," she said phlegmatically.

Sixteen pointed to a group of Dhuur trees in the near distance. The bark of the trees was a rich charcoal black, sticking out in the dusty sandscape. "We could use those trunks. I have a small axe."

The trees were falling together in a circle like a pack of wolves mourning a lost comrade at dawn. Isra glanced at the trees tearily, their shape reminiscent of her own feelings. Sixteen went over to the trees holding the axe. A hyena howled in the distance. He threw the axe at one of the trunks, the blade slipping through the wood with ease. He then chopped at the base of the trunk until it fell to the ground, narrowly missing his toes. He tried to pick the trunk up but felt weak.

"There is a rope in my bag. Can you bring it over?" he croaked.

"What?" Mary replied.

Sixteen made a gesture with his hands of rope being tied. Isra watched the scene, unable to add a voice to the proceedings. She wanted to help but could muster no life within her bones. Watching Sixteen toil with the tree trunk was like watching Amiin, toiling with a fish net on the beach on a scorching hot day. The scene was sad yet amusing.

Mary found the rope and brought it over to Sixteen. He tied the rope to one end of the log, threw the rope over his shoulder and heaved the log along the ground. Despite its dead appearance it was still cumbersome.

"I'll get the axe," Mary said.

"Thank you."

He toiled over the ground with the sun beating down. He took small steps, shuffling at a tortoise's pace. But he was determined to reach the grave, by any means.

The stretch took over ten minutes, Sixteen was exhausted once the log was on top of the grave. He took a sip of water and rolled the black log gently onto the disturbed earth;

realising more logs would be needed. Even then, the desert animals could find a way to dig around the area.

Isra grinned at the solitary log, bent out of shape like a car wheel on the side of the road. "Not going to make a lot of difference, is it?"

Sixteen nodded, grinning broadly back. He spat sand onto the ground. "We can find some boulders. Maybe that would be a better deterrent?"

"And how are we going to get a boulder over here?" Isra replied.

"Rope and muscle?"

Isra smiled again, a light encompassing her eyes. A moisture filled her face, filling her cheeks with beauty. "Since when did you have muscles?"

"Here" Sixteen rolled his sleeves up, flexing his reedy biceps. His arms like pallor sticks waving in the air.

"I just saw your attempt at dragging that log!"

Sixteen released his arms. Mary nodded, sighing.

"Sixteen," said Isra.

"Yes, Isra."

"I do appreciate what you are doing…" She turned her back on the grave and sat down, staring at the clouds morphing into mushrooms. "Can we just sit here for a while?"

"If you wish."

Isra took a sip of the water canister, then passed it to Sixteen. "Then we move for the last time. Mary, you were right. We belong on the coast; we have a much better chance there than here. There is fish in the sea… an abundant food supply if we can find a way to yank them out of the sea. We need to set-up somewhere, before the sun takes us for good."

Sixteen stared blankly at Isra. "I was only supposed to bring you to Amiin" – he took another sip of the water – "and I feel like I failed in my mission. I should just go back and find some of my old group."

"They all died, didn't they?" Mary asked.

"I'm not sure."

"Your leader – Aleja?"

"I know he has gone. Bullet between the eyes."

"And his commanders?"

"He only had one who didn't make it."

"What are you afraid of?" Isra asked, her back still turned.

Sixteen glanced at the back of Isra's head, admiring the small plaits at the tip of her bushy hair. He then looked up at a row of clouds morphing into a large set of waves. "Isra, since as long as I can remember that group were like a family to me. Aleja was a father figure. I felt safe in his company, despite his misgivings."

"What misgivings, Sixteen?"

"He beat us, shouted at us. Only since I've been around you, I realise it was not normal."

"Mary?" said Isra.

"Yes."

"Do you still want to return to the coast?"

"I think so. I am just tired is all."

Isra looked at the clouds dissipating into the horizon. She moved the scarf away from her mouth, tapping the ground where Amiin now lay. "Next ant-race is mine," she said triumphantly, then wept through the night.

Early the next morning they packed their rucksacks for the final journey back to the coast. Isra's grief was numbing her body into a cocoon. They moved along like three ghosts, devoid of hope more out of necessity, having little idea if their fate would work out more favourably on a beach or holed up in a cave in the rocky hinterland.

Sixteen knew of a well along the way, hidden among a dense patch of reeds. The water was murky but palatable. He then guided them to a Yeheb bush for the stems to eat and the bark to suck.

As they approached the path that led up the small cliff towards the ocean, Sixteen noticed a red puff in the sky, eastbound to the beach.

"Stop!" he said.

"What is it?" said Mary.

Sixteen pointed to the remnants of a flare, hanging over the defunct harbor to the east.

"I kept seeing those things popping up. Then they disappear. What are they?" Mary asked.

"Flares. It's a signal that a firefight is about to begin somewhere."

"So, what do we do?"

Sixteen stood transfixed at the long trail of smoke that blew down into the sea. "Hang loose for a while. We'll be okay if we avoid the area around it."

"Did you see the ones firing?" Isra asked.

"Only the Italian mercenaries, think it was Italian. I couldn't tell."

Mary threw her rucksack to the ground. "Why are they here?"

"Shale oil I have heard."

"Oil? Here?"

"They are desperate."

"And where will they take it?"

"Across the Arabian Sea I believe. They use it to power generators."

"What is a generator?"

Sixteen could see blinded innocence clouding Mary's stoic countenance. Despite all the bluster, these comments had shown how little knowledge she had of the world outside. "It powers things. You know, electricity."

Mary looked from side to side. "Like cars?"

"Yes cars, and lots of other things."

"What then?"

"All types of things, Mary. You know all that junk in the towns left in big heaps?"

Mary nodded, transfixed by the revelations pouring out of Sixteen's mouth.

"Well, those rusty heaps of metal were once useful machines. Machines that could wash your clothes, dry your hair, even cook your food."

"You are lying!"

"I am not! Why else were they lying on the road?"

Mary kicked at the ground. A stone was stuck in the gravel. She raised her leg further to disrupt the stone. "Cleaning clothes? I thought they were leftover rockets or something. It looked like rubbish, so I didn't pay it much attention."

"Lived a strange life before us. I heard strange stories about glass screens being integral to their way of life. Like shoes and clothes are to us."

Mary gave up on the stone and continued walking up the hill. "I saw these screens in Hajidwali. There was glass everywhere and black leads poking out of the ends like sand-snakes. I cannot really say I understand it."

The panorama beyond the clifftop came within view. Sixteen could smell the salty texture of sea-air tickling his nostrils. The oxygen here felt purer than the desert, it was beyond smell, more of a feeling within the fibres of his lungs. "Let us stop here. I want to check where the flare came from."

"We can use the side of the hill for shelter," Mary said.

"Wait here," he said.

Sixteen took his rucksack off, moving along the cliff path until the residue of red smoke was within sight. The smoke hung in the sky, like a flock of gulls circling a school of fish. His chest tightened; he knew the group who had fired the flare was the same one he had encountered. Why they were coming along the shoreline he was not sure. His hope was that they were going eastbound, towards the tip of the Horn of Africa.

He closed his eyes, hearing the delicate waves lapping against the shore. He thought about Mary and Isra; two delicate souls needing help. *Help? They did not need his help. All he had given them was a corpse.* He looked down at the two of them, sitting dolefully on their rucksacks with shoulders sinking into the sand and a despairing, flushed out look on their faces. He had seen a similar look on the militia. It was tired, beaten down, the broken look of fate crumbling before their very eyes while the earth carried on spinning at a glacial pace.

He thought about his dwindling options. *Stay with the girls or head off lonesome.* But the truth dawned that he had no idea where to go for food or shelter. He had been like a goat on a piece of string his whole life; following Aleja wherever the wind took him. *Did they want him here?* He racked his brain to find a nugget of acceptance from either. He needed fate to decide so took a rusty coin out of his pocket.

"Heads stay, other go," he whispered. Rubbing the coin with his shirt sleeve he looked at the faded imprint; it was the side profile of a man's head, looking haughty, magisterial. He flipped the coin high into the air. The coin landed between two rocks.

He leant down, fishing between the rocks until the coin came up. Headfirst.

"How are we looking?" Mary shouted.

"Hard to tell. Will know a bit more within the hour."

Mary nodded. He looked at her, just a naïve little girl in his eyes. He could have told her if he urinated into the sea it would turn amber, and the sharks would grow legs and walk onto the shore and she would have believed him. He felt for her, knowing nothing of her back-story. *Just another stranger joining another stranger then another stranger until one day they become friends, family even.* He ruminated about his own parents, wondering what they looked like, their slight of touch, the words that would tumble out of their mouths. He had asked Aleja who they were one day, only to be met with a swift backhand to the face.

He stood up and walked down to them. They sat in the same position, looking away from each other. "Right, if we are going to go any further, I need to get to know a bit more about you two."

"What do you need to know?" Mary replied.

"Let us start with you. What is your story, Mary?"

She coiled her hair with her little finger. "What does it matter?"

"Listen, Mary… let us cut to the chase. Or our arrangement needs to end here."

"What do you need to know?"

Sixteen sat down on a patch of loose soil where sea grasses were growing. He picked the grass, chewing on a lump of blades. "So, who was Mousa?"

A spark ignited in her eyes, the kind of spark he had seen in hyenas when suddenly disturbed. "He was my guardian, if you can call him that."

"From what age?"

"Five, I think. It's a bit hazy."

"And before that? Your parents?"

"Died. I don't really remember them."

"Did Mousa not tell you?"

"No."

"Why not?"

"I did ask but he would get angry. Just said they had left me in the wastelands for the jackals."

Sixteen stood back. "Aleja said a similar thing to me."

"About what?"

"My parents leaving me. He'd raised me from the ground."

Isra turned around, smirking.

"What is it?" Mary asked.

"These so-called guardians. Who are they? At least I know what happened to my folk," said Isra.

"What happened to yours?" Sixteen asked.

"Mother died giving birth to me. Father drowned whilst out fishing one day."

Sixteen stroked the back of his shaggy mop of hair. New curls had formed in the salty sea-air. "I see a trend. Maybe our parents were not supposed to look after us. Maybe it was something born in the sand that tells us, and many before and after us would not know or remember our fathers and mothers."

"Do not be so ridiculous! This is just the time into which we are born. Age is not a stone number. The ones before us lived for eighty, one hundred years. But they had lots of fresh food, clean water, and medicine. What do we have to survive? Dry goat bones, stale water and scraps of antiseptics that are not much use now anyway! Hell to all that, our parent's destiny should be here sitting next to us. Survival is a tough nut to crack."

"So, what is your point?" Mary asked.

"My point is not to look too much at a destiny, or even to look back at long, rich lives by the ones before us. What matters is here and now — survival. And unfortunately, our parents, Amiin, Aleja, Mousa, even those damn goats. Their time was up. End of!"

"Isn't that what Mr. Sixteen was saying?"

"My point is simple, Mary. We are all here; breathing, eating, sleeping one minute. Next, we are in the ground ready to pass onto the next host, whatever form that will be."

"She's right," Sixteen closed his eyes, taking a deep breath. "We all must live for now. What else is there? The past is gone. Buried into the ground with all the good and bad memories. Today we start a new chapter."

Mary gazed at Sixteen, narrowing her eyes at him.

He opened his eyes. A bright image, a shield disappearing from Mary's frosty exterior leapt in front of him. Her shoulders were slumped, arms down by her side. She smiled, candidly.

Sixteen moved over to Isra, rubbing her shoulders. "He will not be forgotten you know," he whispered into her ear. "His spirit lives on with every footstep we take, every fire we light, every glimmer from Orion."

She nodded her head into his. His neck felt warm, comforting. He could hear the soft sound of crying as a wet patch emerged on his shoulder.

A plastic packet blew in from the ocean wind. The packet dropped delicately out of the air, landing below his feet. They both looked at the crinkled blue packaging, hugging his toes.

Isra pulled away from Sixteen. "What does it say?"

"I do not know. Can you read?"

"No."

Mary picked up the packet. It had a burnt, grainy texture

around the open rim of the packet. She turned the packet over. "Rim…. Rimmers sna… snacks. Rimmers Snacks."

"Are you making this up?" Isra asked.

"No, that's what it says."

"Since when can you read?"

She smirked wryly. "I picked up a few words here and there…" her eyes pressed against the plastic wrapping "The Che... cheeseist, ta... ta... tastie… tastiest snacks in the. The wor… world."

"Tried this cheese stuff from the goat's milk. Can't say I liked it," Sixteen said.

"Does it say where it came from?" Isra asked.

Mary turned the packet over. "The writing is tiny. I can't make a lot out of it."

Isra grabbed the packet out of Mary's grasp. "Let me see." She looked the packet over, noticing red, yellow fonts intertwined with a picture of a bear, grinning. "Maybe the Afrikaans brought it with their task force?"

Sixteen glanced at them. He felt like he was always learning something new. "Why were they here?"

"Why would anyone else bother turning up here?"

"Oil?"

Isra nodded.

"And did they find any?"

"I am assuming not. Otherwise, we would have bumped into them."

Mary grabbed the packet back from Isra. "Wait. Rimmer's Snacks… a divisi… division. Can't read the rest… something, something… Coven… Coven... Coventry, UK. UK! That is British right?"

"You sure?" said Sixteen.

"Pretty sure that's what it says."

"Pass it here…" He inspected it closely from side to side like an ancient artefact. "This has come a long way. The British are a long, long way away. A different planet even. I wonder if this was eaten in Britain."

"Mary, can you see how old it is?" Isra handed the packet back.

The print was faded. Mary turned the packet over a couple of times, searching for a number. She scrawled her eyes over the packet, repeatedly. "Can't see anything. Think it's blown in from Britain?"

"Possibly," Isra replied.

"But wouldn't that mean it grew arms and legs and swam?"

Sixteen grinned. "Ha! It grew wings and glided across the ocean!"

"Maybe it buried under the earth and popped up here?" said Mary.

"Oh, holy snack packet why did you grace us with your fine presence."

He could see Isra smiling underneath the scarf. "But seriously this stuff can take years to break down."

"Into what?" Mary replied.

"Soil, and the stuff we walk on, the earth."

"So, what happens to it?"

"It will stay here, left on its own. The wind may blow it around the land and back to sea, but it will not break down; not for a hundred years. We could burn it."

"I saw lots of these packets washed up on the shore near Laasqoray," said Isra.

"But… why would you want to eat food out of a packet. That is disgusting, anything could have been in the packet," Mary said.

Sixteen looked at Isra. It seemed like a fair point. "Most food was packaged into packaging."

"But why? It is so unnecessary!"

"I guess they didn't want to expose it to too much air."

Mary shook her head. "What kind of species were these people? Seems so wasteful. All food stops being fresh, doesn't it? No amount of stupid packaging is going to change that."

"But doesn't the food go mouldy quicker if it is exposed?" Isra asked.

"I get wrapping it in cloth, leaving it in colder places. But this plastic stuff seems pointless."

The three argued the theories behind plastic packaging food longevity for hours, until the sun dropped, and the volume of the sea current went up. The night was another clear one, with a full moon.

They set up camp in the same position under the cliff. Isra slept little that night. Amiin's face would appear every time she closed her eyes; his features barely distinguishable from the brother she knew. All she could see were sprouts of curled hair, one eye and his mouth wide open as if he were trying to speak to her. Sixteen watched her flitting in and out of sleep; her beauty exposed under the moonlight like a hibiscus flower changing colour through the day.

He gazed, in wonder. A feeling grabbed his stomach that he had not felt before. A tender, drifting feeling as if he was floating in the middle of the ocean. It stirred in his chest until he was short of breath. Aleja had taught him about the almighty one who had no name, this god, a father in heaven. But he always had the slightest suspicion that this being was little more than a fallacy, a figment of Aleja's imagination. Somebody was looking down on him; it was his parents. He was clueless about how they looked; images changed regularly. But he felt their presence every day. Two beings drifting in the universe somewhere.

At that moment he felt an overwhelming clarity. He did not want to drift on his own. He wanted to drift among the amorphous clouds under his parents' loving scrutiny.

He wanted to float with Isra.

Chapter Seventeen

Three long weeks passed under the rocky cliffs. Three weeks of relative calm for the newly acquainted group. Three weeks quietly working out their next moves in the survival game, as the beautiful azure of the sky radiated longer each day, revealing itself timidly like flowers casually blooming on a cactus.

A daily routine began to take shape.

Mornings spent cleaning clothes, scrubbing pots, gathering firewood. Afternoons looking for food, collecting rainwater.

Sixteen had engineered fishing lines and rudimentary hooks from discarded plastic wire, the results mixed, with grouper fish visiting their dinner plates occasionally. The process was a long, extended one. Setting the lines, waiting for hours for a nudge on the line, going out to sea to bring the catch in. Then finally reeling the lines carefully back in before twilight arrived. Despite the laborious nature both Sixteen and Mary had fun seeing what new sea-creature would pop onto the hook each day.

Sixteen particularly enjoyed seeing Mary's eyes sparkle when the creature surfaced. Her face burst into life, lifting her sunken eyes into a glorious, youthful ascendency. It was like seeing a small child experience tide bubbles for the first time.

One day a small turtle arose out of the water. Mary held the reptile in the palm of her hand, sizing up whether it was ripe for a meal. She stroked the belly and tickled the top of the turtle's shell, waiting for a reaction. After deliberation they decided to send the turtle back into the ocean.

Isra spent the weeks resting, saying little. Her dour expression showed no signs of abating, to the disappointment of Sixteen and Mary. Every afternoon, after lunch she would retreat into the tent and gaze forlorn into the ocean. She would ponder the ocean for hours, with a blank, motionless expression; her hopes and dreams hiding somewhere in the big blue. Sixteen would come back from the shore thinking she had turned into a statue.

Today was a blustery day. A mist had descended, spiralling along the cliff-faces like a thick, dewy spider's web. Sixteen headed back along the shore. "Check the rain sheets, will you?" he said to Mary.

Mary dutifully ran ahead, barely visible from fifty metres ahead. Four plastic sheets were tied between a congregation of palm trees, underneath the cliff edge. The sheets had a slanted edge, angled like a roof. Beneath the sheets a row of plastic bottles lined up, perfectly straight.

"Looks good. One is half full!" she shouted. Her image dotted in and out of the mist, clips of hair, a shoe, the swinging of an arm. Her silhouette then disappeared completely. "How about the other bottles?" Sixteen shouted.

A silence engulfed Sixteen's ears; a deathly silence like a lull in a gunfight. "Mary?" he shouted.

A figure then appeared out of the mist, and Sixteen realised it was too tall to resemble Mary. A dirty, white Salwar Kameez dangled around a languorous body with slumped shoulders. Around the edges of the face blew the long growth of a wispy beard. He turned around with Mary held tightly in his grip. Into the air the figure thrust a knife.

"Hold it there, fiend!" he shrilled.

Sixteen stopped, holding his hands upright. "Don't want any trouble here."

"Who else is with you?"

Sixteen felt the palms of his hands sweating. "Just me and the girl, that's all."

The man stepped forward, with Mary held in his elbow. His hair was pepper-potted brown and white, tied into a loose ponytail. His composure serene, as if he had held hostages before. "Where are you staying?" he asked.

"Not far. What do you want?"

The man moved forward. Sixteen could see sunburns

blotching his forehead and around his eyes, as if a scrap with the sun had beaten his face. He pointed with the blade. "Pass me that bottle."

Sixteen moved forward, crouched under the sheet, and collected the bottle. He thought how that water could have kept him hydrated for days.

The man snatched the bottle. "Thank you." He gulped all the water down.

Whether it was the long-straggled hair, the wispy beard. He looked familiar to Sixteen. "Tell you the truth I am on the run. If I let the girl loose, you won't scream to the heavens, will you?"

"There is nobody around here."

"You are sure?"

"Well, I did see a red flare a few weeks ago."

The man's face clenched. "A red flare? In which direction?"

"Eastern shore. Do you know what it is?"

The man released Mary from his grasp. Mary reciprocated by giving his arm a bite.

"Ouch!" the man screamed.

"Next time I'll bite your testicles off!" She ran towards Sixteen.

The man inspected the bite mark. He grinned, devilishly. "What do you want to know?"

"Where are they coming from? What do they mean?"

"What?"

"The flares."

The man edged closer. Out of his back pocket came a bag of chaat, he scooped a lump out and threw it in his mouth. "The flares you do not need to worry about, friend."

Sixteen could feel his shoulders relaxing. "Why? Tell me about them."

"The flares… the flares… ha! Merely symbolic. Call it a warning signal not to go there."

Mary emerged behind Sixteen's right leg "Who is there? Monsters?"

"Monsters! Ha! It depends on the interpretation."

"Come on quit the jibber. Who is it?"

The man spat chaat on the ground, then wiped his mouth with his dirty sleeve. Sixteen could see red chaat stains in his thick, mangled beard. "There are two factions at play. One is a coalition between the Russo and the Arabians. Another is a group from the Mediterranean. They are warning each other off with the flares."

"Warning each other from what... is it oil?"

The man stopped chewing; his face dropped. "Oil you say? How do you know such things?"

"Just what I've heard."

The man laughed, then continued chewing. "You are not far wrong. Devil's blood I call it. There is also natural gas in the ground."

"Is it like treasure?" Mary interjected.

"What?"

"The oil."

"Treasure? Some folk called it the black gold. All I saw was a trickily mess that caused a lot of death."

"What did they use it for?"

"It came out of the ground, like water out of a well. They then put it into barrels and used ships to get it across the Arabian Sea. From there it took a longer journey through Arabia where they would burn it to light fires and make things out of."

"Can't they just burn wood for their fires?"

The man stroked the end of his beard, like he was stroking a cat. "This oil has a special property in it I believe. I heard it was like a spirit that ascended to the heavens."

"And you are on the run from these bandits?"

The man spun on the spot, holding his arms aloft. "Ten points to the girl!"

Sixteen walked away from the man.

"Where are you going?" the man asked.

"Back to our camp. Don't think we need to know anymore."

"And where is that?"

"Never mind."

The man shuffled awkwardly onto one foot, studying the ground. "I just wanted someone to talk to. Been on the road for months."

Sixteen turned around. The scraggy ends of the Salwar Kameez were scrapping along the rocky floor, hiding his leather sandals where two green bulbous toes poked out at strange angles. The nails jagged like hawk talons; talons that hung loosely from the sickly toes. Sixteen's gaze was drawn to a tattoo on the stranger's left wrist; some kind of scripture; two lines moved over what appeared to be the sun with a head in between.

"What's that on your wrist?"

"This?" He stroked his wrist. "From Italia, my friend. Was part of a brotherhood, a religious brotherhood."

Suspicions started to grow. He thought back to the firefight which punctured his dreams. *Who were the bandits who invaded them that night? Their accents sounded similar to the stranger.*

"What's your name?"

"Mauricio. You can call me Mau."

Mauricio. He thought Isra had mentioned that name before; A crazy old man wandering the desert in his robes. A man who had travelled all the way from Europe, and nobody knew why. Isra had talked fondly of this enigma.

Sixteen glanced at Mary. "Fill the rest of the bottles."

He continued to walk slowly along the shore. The sea suddenly muted as Mauricio joined him by his side. As he felt Mauricio's presence closer to his hip a prickly sensation welled up in his chest.

"Tell me more about this group you escaped from."

Mauricio kept pace with Sixteen, swinging his arms wildly. Sixteen could hear his shallow breathing. "I ran into them close to here, in the hinterland, about a year ago. As soon as they heard my accent, they knew I would be useful, so they kidnapped me and sent me to work in a house near Hajidwali."

"What did they make you do?"

"Cleaning out metal barrels. Stinky, mucky stuff it was. Can still smell the chemical stench in my fingers."

"Who were they?"

"European mainly, with a few stragglers from the Djibouti area."

"And they were here for oil?"

Mauricio slowed down, clutching his chest. "Slow down a bit, will you?"

Sixteen stopped. He clutched Mauricio's skinny shoulders. "Are you okay?

"Yes, that stuff just got stuck in my lungs is all."

"So, it was oil?"

Mauricio nodded. "They were trying to expand into the hinterland."

Sixteen paced slowly. "Why?"

"They had tip-offs of oil fields close by, twenty, thirty miles inland. The only problem was other clans also had the tip-offs. You cannot underestimate how valuable this stuff is to the clans across the seas. They use it to power machines, drive trucks, make all kind of things."

"Other clans?"

"There was the Russo/Arabian clan. An alliance of white and brown skins. I never saw them firsthand, but they were supposed to be a nasty lot. Had nasty weapons that would make you go blind. Then there was this other ragtag lot we ran into many weeks ago. Young they were, looked local. Bit like you, actually."

Sixteen's chest tightened like his lungs were pinching his heart. "I was."

"You were what, friend?"

"You heard me. I was there."

Mauricio scratched the side of his head. Sixteen could see tiny twigs falling out of his matted hair. He turned his face towards the ground. "Oh. I am sorry, friend. I did not know."

"Your bunch took a sizable chunk out of my group that day. I remember it vividly. The flare; the commotion, the gunshots, explosions."

Mauricio's eyes shined hazy green as the sun glistened off the ocean. A haunted look blew across his face. "We were under orders. Was terrible what they made us do. All they said was pass through your group even if white flags went up. Steam past them or get shot yourself."

Sixteen felt a tear welling up in the corner of his eye. The young men who died that day had stayed with him, and he now felt guilty. Some of them were his friends, bodies perishing in the heat as the vultures toured the skies, licking their gunshot wounds, howling into the mist of gunshot residue. But they were gone, and he was still here. And something in his bones convinced him the same old man had done nothing wrong, paradoxically.

"Did you kill any?"

Mauricio kept his gaze on the ground, seashells had washed up on the shore. "They made me fire at your group, but I just fired around. I'm hoping the shots didn't hit bone, but I can't be sure."

Sixteen snapped his head at Mauricio. The curls of his hair blew briskly against the wind, revealing a weather-beaten face for the world to see. He saw a broken man staring at the ground, wishing for compassion. Aleja, Mousa, the clans all sounded the same to him. All complicit in their own devilish coercing of young bodies for their own selfish greed. Aleja told him that the human brain could be moulded into any shape from birth, unlike the other animals, making them the ultimate intelligent species. He now saw how this was carved into manipulation.

He showed Mauricio to the top of the cliff. "Come with me."

Mary emerged behind them carrying three bottles.

"Where are we going?" Mauricio asked.

"There is someone you might know."

They moved down the grassy slope to the encampment.

Isra was hanging a pair of cotton trousers out to dry. At first, she ignored the movement over the cliffs, safe knowing who it was. She looked over again. The stuttering walk of Mauricio, his body silhouetting against the clouds like a beachside painting. The wind lifted the sides of his long hair and Isra knew instantly who it was.

She ran towards Mauricio. "Mau! Is that you?"

Chapter Eighteen

"Isra! Is that you?"

Mary looked on. "Care to tell me who this guy is?"

Isra wiped tears away from her eyes; seeing Mauricio was like seeing Amiin reincarnated before her. Despite the greying hair and longer beard he was recognisable, like a living fossil. She suddenly felt a tint of joy. "Who is this guy… he's only Mauricio the king of La corsa dei nostril tempi!"

"La corsa what?"

"The Race of our Times. Ant racing. I will teach you someday."

She took a step away from Mauricio. A shy smile creeped out of his mouth. "Can't believe you are here, Mau. Where have you been? I thought you were dead."

Mauricio took a fresh lump of chaat out of the bag. "Been a few places. It is good to see you, Isra. Last time you were very little. I am surprised you recognise me! Where is your brother?"

She nodded. The kind of sideways nod to suggest.

"He has gone?"

She looked out to the sea, a tear forming in her eye. "Didn't make it."

He took a step away from Isra, staring out to sea, deferential. "I am sorry to hear that. Really sorry. He was a wonderful young man."

"He was shot by the Europeans or the Russo or whoever they were…" Sixteen interjected "We both managed to escape but the wound got him in the end."

Mauricio sat on a rock, breathing heavily. "Accidenti! I can't believe our groups crisscrossed into death in such a way. Stronza's! It was not me, Isra, please believe me. Some of those guys just wanted to kill. Would have eaten the flesh; they were so hungry."

She sat next to Mauricio, looking at the cliff-face, forlorn. Her hand touched his shoulder. "I believe you, Mau. How did you escape?"

Mauricio put the ball of chaat into his mouth wiping his hands on the rock. "I just ran one day, as fast as I could when they were all sleeping."

"Will they come looking for you?"

"I do not know."

Sixteen and Mary stood upright against the cliff wall, looking intently at Isra for a signal. Isra embraced Mauricio, holding him tight against her chest. As she did the laps of waves from the shore delicately brushed against her ears. A subtle, hushed sound. "You can stay with us if you like," she whispered into his ear.

"What do you think she is saying?" Mary asked.

"She's asking him to join us," Sixteen replied.

"Another mouth to feed? Really?"

"I think he can be a good addition. He is a man of many worlds. Who knows maybe we can set sail across the sea?"

Mary looked out to the shore and the endless horizon. "Would you want to?"

"The sea… why not?"

"But this land is all we know."

Sixteen smirked, his eyes lowered to Mary's shoulders. Right now, she was a newborn baby. "Mary, child. Eventually, we are going to run into those groups that want the oil, and then what?"

"They won't be interested in us, will they?"

"Of course they will. They will take whatever hostages they can. That is what happened with my group. Aleja thought that the more boys he could collect the more chance he would have of survival. Amiin was a hostage."

"That makes no sense, though. More food, water, clothes, shoes. Surely, he could not provide for every stranger he picked up."

"It is a numbers game. The weaker ones he would leave by the side for the almighty one to provide for. While the strongest would march with him into battle."

She threw a stone up the hill. "This battle talk sounds so exhausting. Why can't we all just mind each other's business? That was what me and Mousa did."

The stone hit a rock face and tumbled down the hill. "You have answered your own question there, Mary."

"What question?"

"Why you do not want to sail."

Mary picked another stone off the ground, this time throwing it over the cliff towards a rock-pool on the other side. "It is the unknown I suppose. We do not know what is across the sea do we?"

"Has to be better than this, though, doesn't it?"

"But this is our home. And this is our way of life."

"Our home? Do we have such a thing?"

Isra stood up suddenly. "Mary, Sixteen, can you come over?"

Mary waited for Sixteen to get up, then moved towards Isra.

"I am putting this to a vote. Who would be happy with Mauricio here staying with us?"

"How long for?" Mary asked.

"As long as he wishes. Mau?"

"As long as you want me," Mauricio replied. "I can get us some supplies."

Sixteen brushed his hair out of his face. "What about out there?" He pointed to the sea.

"What about it?" Mauricio replied.

"What is out there?"

He smiled incredulously. "Lots of water, my friend!"

"The land I mean. The land!"

"Since when did this become an option?" Isra asked.

Sixteen focused onto Isra. He fixed his head straight at her, focusing on the freckles around her cheeks. "Isra, how long will it be before they find us? And then what? More toils with another gang moving in and out of the desert looking for God knows what. The desert may have been our enslavers, but this would be much worse, being in the hands of another Mousa or an Aleja, and I do not want that. We are tough, Isra, but not that tough. Now is the time to go across the sea."

Isra looked away from Sixteen. Clouds were beginning to float in from the west. She turned to Mauricio. "What is there, across the sea, Mau?"

Mauricio picked a stone off the floor. He spat on the stone and rubbed it with his shirt sleeve. "You see this? Know where it came from?"

"A stone."

"Ah! But it is not just a stone, Isra. This very stone probably came out of a volcano when these two lands were joined together."

She looked at Sixteen, perplexed. "And your point is?"

Mauricio gazed out to a dip in the cliff where he could see the sea, sparkles shapeshifting. "That is my point, Isra. This land was once the land of Arabia, connected with the great African continent. What is out there? There is sand, great deserts, deserted communities and danger, obvious danger. But there are also tools to start over again, Isra. Many, many tools. And a bit of hope. This land has gone. All that is left are a few scraps of minerals to fight over. I agree with Sixteen, let nature take the land over again, let it flourish without us. We both don't need each other."

Mary picked a stone off the ground. She held it carefully. Examining the patches of moss on one side. "But this is all we know. How do we know there is not another trap out there waiting for us. What about the pirates of the Arabian Sea?"

"I cannot guarantee anything," said Mauricio. "As for pirates, I do not know. I have not heard sightings of pirates for some time."

Sixteen and Mary looked at Isra intently. "I am tired. Can we think about it over the night?" Isra said.

Sixteen shrugged. "We need to make a decision very soon, before it is too late."

"One night. That is all I am asking."

Mauricio threw the stone to the top of the cliff. "Well, whatever you decide I am going to start finding wood. I have made my mind up and I want to take my chances across the sea. I miss the fresh, salty sea air and the stillness of the ocean. I miss seeing dolphin fins poking out of the water surface and the sun setting unparalleled against the backdrop of blue land, shifting ever so slightly into the twilight. And I miss laying on my back and watching the stars float aimlessly by while the waves lap gently against my ears."

Isra spent the evening on the beach, watching the waves lapping against her feet while the others prepared to sleep. The evening was a mild one, with a cooling breeze brushing the side of her face. She spent hours thinking about the blank face of her mother. About Amiin. About Mousa's depraved acts. And her own future. The thoughts jumbled around her head; listlessly bumping into one another like the seeds of plants colliding with the soil. Her mood was sombre, thinking about the ones who were not here to advise. *For what did she really know about Mary, Sixteen and Mauricio? They had all drifted in together from various places but what were their real motives?*

She too was now questioning what to do with her own future. Amiin's loss still pierced her heart every day, like a spike slowly delving into the soft tissue of her innermost feelings. *What was the point in continuing without him?* She got to her feet; her strength was waning, and dizziness overcame her so she sat down again. Inside her chest a melancholia gripped her rib-cage tight, so tight she could feel herself suffocating from the inside. And while her chest gripped tight a sour taste rolled around the underside of her tongue, a taste like jackal meat souring. She spat on the sand while the waves cascaded around her ears. Pain, eating her from the inside.

As the last ray of twilight escaped from the horizon, she felt a hopelessness swimming around her body. The feeling numbed every muscle until she could almost feel her final heartbeat. Inside her trouser pocket she felt the knife that had slain Mousa. She took the knife out and felt the smooth metal of the blade as the darkness descended not just on the beach but her whole body, weighing down on her shoulders like a gigantic boulder. *I will not have to make a decision. This could be over very soon. I can join you, dear brother, dear mother.* Something about the blade felt warm and inviting as the silver illuminated against the chalky skin on her fingers. The blade suddenly multiplied in her hands; two, three, four times. She tossed it from hand to hand. The blade multiplied like a fan; ten, fifteen, twenty times. Her head skipped uncontrollably against the hush beat of the waves, trying to adjust her vision.

"Stop playing tricks on me! Is this your way to say use me? You silly piece of metal! I know what you are saying. No need for tricks." She raised the twenty blades into the air, the tip braising the edge of Orion's last star. She nodded at the stars, in acknowledgement of the final function as her heartbeat slowed.

The twenty blades suddenly disappeared into the sky. She closed her eyes, waiting for Amiin's words. Out of the corner of her eye Sixteen's face appeared, covering the final star with a benign expression. The blades were thrown to the ground, and he leant down and embraced Isra. He held her tight, squeezing the last drop of hopelessness out of her until his lips met her and they kissed. At first, she pulled away, staring deep into Sixteen's burning retinas. She wanted to see if the same droplets of maddening lust that Mousa had were somewhere hiding amongst the jelly. She stared evermore into his caring eyes; darkened pearls lighting up the beach like electric lamps on a dusty road. He came over to her and stroked the side of her head. "What are you doing, Isra?"

"I don't know," she replied. "Hold me, please."

He gripped her by the shoulders, pressing her nose into his chest. She smelt Sixteen's chest; it smelt like Amiin's. He moved his head to the side and went to kiss her on the lips. This time she locked her lips into his and gently moved her tongue inside of his mouth. She tasted oily fish on his breath and a tinge of salty sea water. There was another taste she could not put her finger on, an enigmatic flavour. He moved his lips away looking deep into her eyes; a flower was about to blossom inside, one of such irresistible colour and beauty that made him cry. "I love you, Isra." He pulled her head into his shoulder.

Isra looked out into the sea where dolphin fins cast shadows against the moonlight. She concentrated on the sounds of the night, noticing the howls of hyenas had gone. Replaced by the seductive hushing of the waves and Sixteen's thumping heartbeat. "Let's go," she said, still facing outwards.

"Go where?"

"Let's build that boat and cross the sea."

Sixteen kissed Isra on the side of her head. He then looked down at the blade lying in the sand. He kicked it into the sea, still holding onto Isra. The knife disappeared underneath a small wave.

Isra moved her head towards Sixteen's ear. "What was that you kicked?"

"Nothing. I was just kicking away the old and starting with the new."

Chapter Nineteen

The boat building commenced in the morning, under the instruction of Mauricio. Sixteen and Mauricio awoke early to scour the beach for driftwood with limited success. They moved into the outskirts of the hinterland where Acacia's, Date Palm's and Pencil Cedar's stood. The wood was not the most durable but was the best they could find. They chopped at the young trees with a make-shift axe made of a sharp piece of flint tied to a plastic tube. And slowly they brought the wood back to the beach on their shoulders.

The light was beginning to fade. Sixteen looked back at Mauricio along the road towards the coast, his feet lumbering along the gravel.

"One thing I was meaning to ask you, Mau."

"Questions... always so many questions, Mr. Sixteen."

Mauricio dropped the Pencil Cedar trunk. "If you must..."

Sixteen dropped the thicker trunk of Date Palm and turned to face him. "Your story.... Where does it start? How did you end up in Africa?"

Mauricio scooped a piece of chaat from his pocket. He placed the chaat delicately into the side of his mouth. "Italia is where it began for me...." He looked past Sixteen's shoulders, focusing on a vulture chewing the corpse of a desert mouse on the side of the road. "It was once a great land; I mean for heaven's sake it was where the Roman Empire started! By the time I set sail on the Mediterranean it was a broken country. Too many people, not enough food, medicine. Vacant buildings, no order. The bird virus was the final straw. It wiped out whole settlements."

"Bird virus?"

He sat on a boulder, playing with the strands of his hair. "The virus came out of the sky; they think it was the pigeons. Once the virus made its way into the humans there was no cure, and no medical care. No hope. The Christian Brotherhood came knocking to my abode one day, saying they were going to set up a commune along the River Nile. I had nothing to keep me in Italia so took the first boat from Sicily. The journey was treacherous, but it taught me about naval matters… sails, winds, currents. I even learned how to survive hyperthermia."

"But I thought the European lands were the promised lands? Plentiful food, clean water. Houses as far as the eye could see with proper roofs, heating."

"Tuh! Many years ago, my boy. Did you ever think about going north?"

"Aleja warned against it. He said war amongst the clans was brutal."

"He is not far off. When man is fighting for the last crumb of bread or drop of water brutality can take over, animal instinct. And there are many people fighting for the scraps."

He sighed, spitting chaat on the ground. "I hear Arabia is more civilised. We will be okay."

"Were the Arabs not hooked up with the Russo. Looking for the oil?"

"Once we get across the sea, they won't be interested in us. The minerals under the land are what they crave. They found copper and nickel deposits in the Horn of Africa a few years ago. I do not know if it was a big find but it was enough for the clans of the north to come prospecting. You see, the black gold, the oil, had almost dried up. And I cannot state, Mr. Sixteen, how essential this resource was to the old way of life. It powered their machines and kept economies working. It developed technology to do things we can only dream of…" he stared intently beyond Sixteen's shoulder, touching his mouth.

"But it also led to tremendous conflict between the clans. Mass slaughter, hunger, disease. It nearly ended the journey of man, woman and child that I was told. But that is the old way and this the new way. A chance to forge a new path."

"I hope so, Mau. It would be nice to have hope."

"There is always hope. The Brotherhood taught me that" – he paused, scratching his forehead nervously – "that was before one of the clans came running through us. A horrid clan from far north, Scandinavia I believe it was. They were hungry, very hungry. Let us not get into detail about human flesh."

"They ate your brothers' flesh?"

He nodded, a tear welling up in the side of his eye. "Luckily, I didn't taste so good."

Sixteen looked around at the vulture, hacking away at the last scrap of sinew on the mouse's body. Nothing surprised him anymore.

They returned to the cliffs within the hour, exhausted. Both fell asleep quickly.

In the morning, they slowly chopped the wood into poles, tying them together with dried seaweed. Over the weeks they added another layer of tied poles and filled the gaps with wood shavings and moss from the rocks. Cushions were made from discarded jumpers lying on the beach, pumped full of gull feathers.

Mauricio kicked at the mainframe of the raft. It was sturdy, if unpretty.

He had grand visions of a boat with a beautiful bow and a fifteen-foot sail, but time was of the essence. However, he was not prepared to travel without a good set of oars, so days were spent carving the oars from cedar wood to exact dimensions, with carved grips and extra moss added to the handles, to avoid sores.

"Does she have a name?" Isra asked.

"Who says it's she?" Mauricio replied.

"Just a feeling, Mau. She is a beautiful piece of work."

Mauricio inspected one side of the raft, where a loose end of seaweed stuck out. He cut it loose with a bite. "Yeah, she's not bad for a few weeks work, I'll give myself that."

"Canab. We shall call her."

"Canab. A grape?"

Isra smiled. "Yes."

"Why Canab?"

"It was my mother's name. Not that I knew her."

"Canab it is then. I am sure Amiin would approve."

Sixteen appeared, carrying three plastic cups. "Here," he passed the cups to Mauricio and Isra.

"You two are full of surprises today! What is it?" Isra asked.

"It is tea. My own special brew of herbs, bush plant."

Isra took a sip. "Sixteen's special brew, not that bad!"

Mauricio's countenance twitched. He tied his hair behind one ear with his left hand. "Hmmm," he slurred.

"Not up to your high standards?" said Sixteen.

"You can have mine, Isra." Mauricio fumbled around in his jacket pocket, he looked at Isra. "Did you fill the cannisters with the rest of the boiled water?"

She nodded.

"Then there is one last thing we need to do. A decision needs to be made."

Sixteen and Isra looked at each other blankly.

Mauricio smirked. "We must decide who is going to row the first leg. We are a democracy, aren't we?"

They both nodded.

Mary then appeared behind Mauricio, holding a large cedar log. Mauricio revealed a ball of tissue paper from his pocket. He unfolded the paper gently. "Only one way to decide."

They peered inside the paper where four large ants were crawling from side to side. "A final game before we set sail. Who do you bet on?"

"Ants?" Sixteen asked, confused.

Isra's face beamed with joy. It was like the whole of her life had been leading up to this one, joyous moment. "Ants! The race of our times, Sixteen. The race!"

"You mentioned this silly game before. How do you play it?"

"Pick an ant. They race each other. It's that simple."

Sixteen sighed. He knew that he would end up with the lame ant and that he would do most of the rowing. Turning towards Isra, he gazed longingly at the twinkles that appeared, slight twinkles of glistening starlight's that danced around the emerald palette that had grown brighter with each day. Isra took the bandana off her forehead, revealing freckles around the tops of her eyebrows and a whole mane of wild, untouched hair.

"I'll take that one," he pointed at the smaller one with a copper tinge.

Mauricio, with an excitable devilment in his eyes turned to Isra. She examined each one by letting them crawl onto her index finger and looking at them closely. One of the ants crawled quickly along the nail of her finger. "This one looks like a winner. My prize-ant."

"I'll take the darker one," Mary said.

"Very well. Follow me." Mauricio carefully cradled the ants in his closed hands.

The racetrack was set up behind two big boulders, near a rock pool. "How long have you been making this?" Isra asked, looking at the intricate racetrack.

The border of the track was made of wispy reeds woven in between small sticks stacked up to one foot. The ground was covered in a fine, white sand, like the sand of the desert, carved into four lanes by barriers of plastic boxes fabricated to even heights.

"So, what happens? They just make a run for it?" Sixteen asked.

"We give them a gentle nudge and let them go on their way. Only time we can disturb the race is if they climb out of their lane. Then we pick them up and put them back where they left the track."

"But they will be crawling all over the place; how on earth will they run in a straight line?"

"Exactly! You bet on the one who goes forward rather than sideways. It can take a while."

"Oh, Mau, it has been so long since I played this. Last time I beat Amiin he was not happy!" Isra said.

"So, we don't bet on anything but pure chance that one of these little critters will go straight?" Sixteen asked.

"Pretty much," Isra said. "That is the beauty of the ant-race. You think you have it all figured out by the look of the ant; strong legs, longer antennae or a colour that just screams fast. Then they easily deceive you. I swear they do it on purpose, just to remind us that nature can't be understood so easily."

"Ninety million years they have been around," Mauricio said.

"Descended from wasps, are they not?" Isra replied.

"How do you know that?" Sixteen interjected.

"They look like wasps if you look at them closer. Wasps are just big flying ants."

"Well, I am learning something today."

"Let us begin the race," Mauricio shouted.

Mauricio brought his cupped hands towards Isra who opened her clutch slightly until her racer neatly cupped within her grasp. He then gestured to Sixteen and Mary to do the same. Sixteen struggled to get the tiny insect under control, he flapped his fingers, getting the ant within his grasp.

"When I say go, release your racer onto the track," Mauricio bellowed.

Isra and Sixteen exchanged glances. Sixteen sensed something changing in the air once the race was over. This race he knew was futile, for the outcome was irrelevant no matter which one finished first. What felt different was a sense of hope, optimism blowing in off the sea and into his nostrils. The smell was like nothing he had smelt before; not salty, dry, aromas. Not a smell that went away or hit his nostrils intensely. It was a smell that lingered ever so gently since Mauricio had called La corsa dei nostril tempi. And he knew who was fanning the faint smell his way. It was Isra.

"C'mon, you beauty, you can do it! You can do it!" she yelped.

"GO!" Mauricio shouted.

The ants were released. Sixteen looked on as his racer jerked forward in a perfect straight line like an arrow. He looked at the other three trailing behind his. Isra's moved diagonally, ending up feeling around the side of the wall while Mauricio's went backwards before getting a nudge from his thumb. Mary's decided to freeze on a comfortable piece of sand.

Sixteen's continued to pace forward, its antennae feeling the way forward in a straight line. It then suddenly stopped, inspecting a piece of grit. "C'mon move. That way!" Sixteen pointed at the finishing line where a piece of string hung loosely from two sticks. "C'mon!"

Isra and Mary shrieked incessantly, while Mauricio calmly watched from the side with arms folded.

Isra's now started to move forward with some speed and was fast catching up to Sixteen's. Mary's brought the rear up with slow, sludgy movements. Just in front was Mauricio's, who was gathering a quick pace. Sixteen moved to the side of the track and waved the racer forward while Isra screamed at the top of her voice that rattled Sixteen's eardrums. For a spilt second, he thought he was back in a gunfight.

From the corner of his eye Sixteen could see Isra's gaining ground rapidly while his continued to poke around a mound of gravel. "Move! Move!" he shouted, flapping his hands wildly.

The racer suddenly moved in a diagonal trajectory towards the finishing line, a foot in front. Sixteen glanced at Isra's, centimeters from his. He then glanced over to where Mauricio's was staggering forwards at a rate of knots towards the finishing line. It was now a three-way race, with Sixteen's just in front and Mauricio's just behind Isra's. Sixteen yelped for his racer to move faster just as Isra's overtook his. As Isra's overtook it stopped in the middle of the track and felt around the sand with its antennae.

Sixteen shrugged. His race was over.

Isra urged her racer towards the finishing line, now inches

away. But Mauricio's racer had now gathered speed, hurtling towards the line.

"Going to be close this," Sixteen shouted into Mary's ear.

"C'mon, my boy, you can do it. Only a few steps, just a few!"

Mauricio calmly looked on. His racer was now right up to the rear of Isra's. He then raised his left arm into the air, like he was signalling to the ant. The racer passed Isra's and blitzed its body past the string and up the side of a boulder. Mauricio's arm swung down by his side, the ant disappearing behind a rock. The race was over.

"How did that happen, little thing? You had the race won!" Isra shouted, excitement still in her lungs. Sweat beads had formed around the side of her forehead, a heart shape that shone in the sunshine.

Sixteen looked down at the ant, standing still in the middle of the track. The pigment had turned pink under the sun with the exertion. He laughed. "It's okay, Mary, I knew it. It was written in the stars I'd be taking the first leg."

He looked over to Mauricio looking down deadpan at the track.

"Fancy a re-match when we get over the other side?" Isra asked, watching the ant crawl over the boulder.

"How do you know there will be ants over the sea?" Sixteen asked.

Isra turned to Mauricio. "Mau?"

"We are not going to Mars!" He nodded. "I see this as a good omen. If one of the ants decides to move straight towards the end like it has a purpose then we have a purpose, my friends. For La corsa dei nostri tempi is not just a simple race between insects. You can sense from the race how your upcoming journey will be. And this be a fortuitous journey, I can feel it, my friends!"

Sixteen nodded at Mauricio. Recognition that this was a new world they would be entering, first the unpredictable sea and then the land of Arabia. But it was a land that would be made of rock, have air to breathe and where ants would live. Isra carefully took the boulders away from the track and cut the string. "There you go, the race of our times is over, and you must row the first part. Great, isn't it?" she turned to Sixteen.

"It's okay, I can handle a bit of rowing."

"I can help you when your arms are tired," Mary said.

Sixteen grinned, and a flash of light lit his tongue "I always knew I would be. I do not mind." He knelt down towards Isra and hugged her from behind. She put her hand on his shoulder, feeling safe. A warmth travelled between their two bodies, sending tickles of laughter through their throats.

Later that afternoon as the seagulls cawed the evening call Isra looked out to the horizon. The clouds had parted, leaving a neat blue road to the sun. She turned away from the sun. A drop of sweat dropped to the ground near where the race had taken place. She looked down to where the drop had fallen, a group of pebbles in low tide. The pebbles had algae blotches that glowed verdantly in the diminishing light. She sat down, waiting for the waves to encircle her feet.

Amiin's shadow appeared in front of her for a fleeting moment, clutching a stick. He waved the stick towards the sea, then disappeared. She looked down at the pebbles, now covered in foamy water and thought about the day when the red light first appeared.

Sixteen and Mauricio heaved the raft out into the tide. They both looked like giants, pushing a huge ship into the sea. "Ready?" Sixteen said.

Isra nodded, looking down at the waves brushing against her feet. The water was warm.

The raft slowly made its way onto the waves and away from the shore, bobbing. Isra stared at the very spot where the last drop of sweat had fallen amongst the algae pebbles. The shadow of the flat shoreline against the hill silhouetted against the navy sky where thick clouds were enveloping the land. And in the far distance she saw a red speck of light, pinging towards the evening star of Venus. The seagull call faded and Isra turned towards the sun where the navy streaks were clear.

"Nabad gelyo." Sixteen waved.

"Goodbye, old friend," said Mauricio. "La corsa dei nostril tempi!"

A distant hyena yelp reverberated briefly around the cliffs. Isra smiled as a tear dropped from her eyes into the darkened, blissful sea. The teardrop rippled around the boat as the sun finally set below the brow of the hill on the shore of the land. The land she was now leaving behind.

Alex Conway was born in 1978 in Luton, Bedfordshire.

He served in the British Army between 1997-2000 and was based in Paderborn, Germany.
During his service he was involved in two tours of the Balkans region: serving in Bosnia–Herzegovina and Kosovo.

He now lives in London, working in brand licensing. His first novel *Destiny: 0422* was published in 2020.

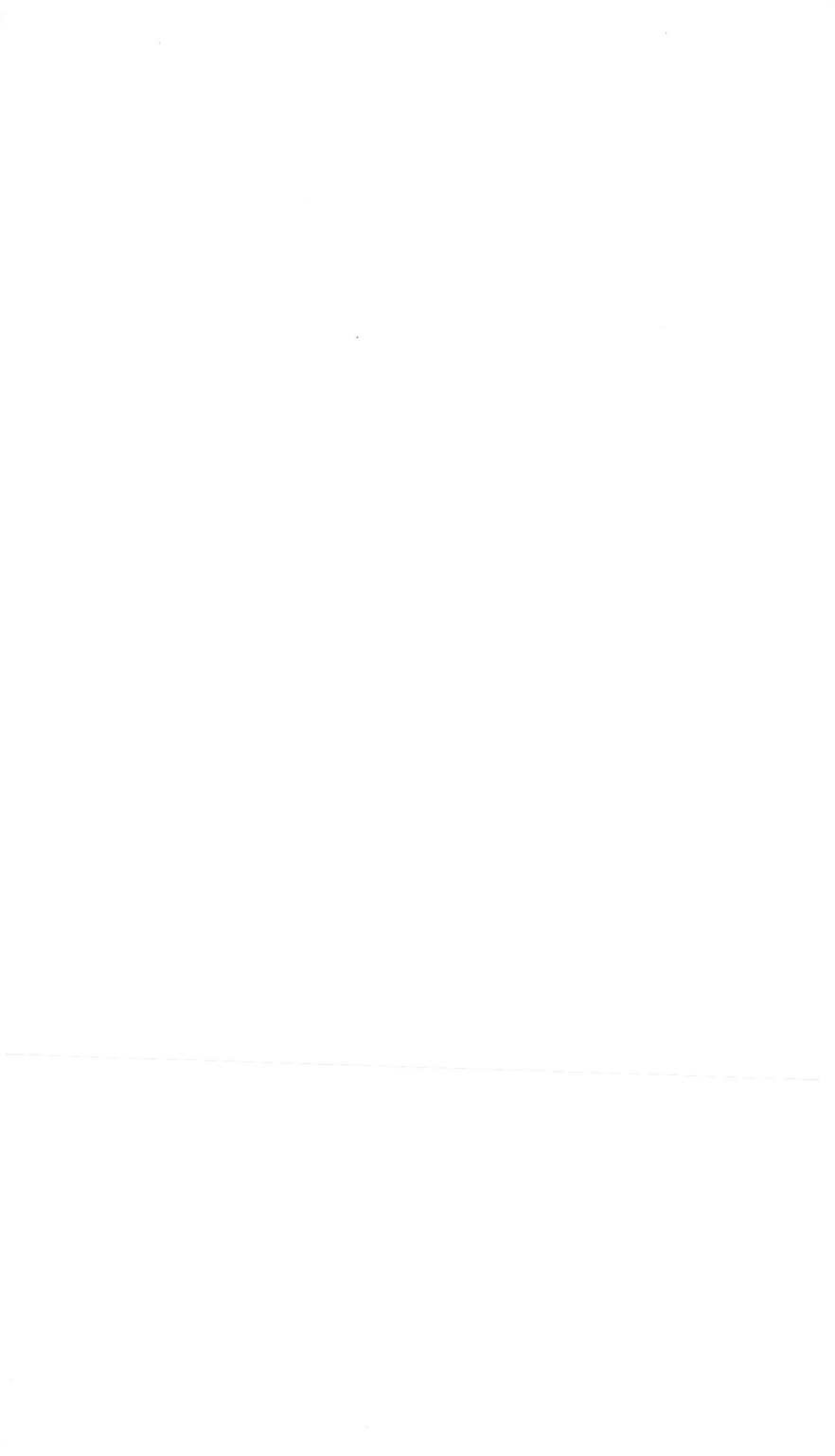